SHiFT

AN ANTHOLOGY

Naomi Artemi

Devin Hunt

Cheyenne Shaffer

Eric Sterbenk

Kyle Thompson

Keegan Young

INK ALCHEMY
BOOKS

AN INK ALCHEMY BOOKS ORIGINAL

Compilation copyright © 2024 by Ink Alchemy Books

The stories which comprise this anthology are works of fiction. Names, characters, places, and incidents either are the product of the authors' imaginations or are used fictitiously. Any resemblance to actual persons, living or dead, events, or locales is entirely coincidental.

Trade Paperback ISBN: 979-8-9906798-2-5

Cover Art by Nikki Morgan

inkalchemybooks.com

For my parents, David & Christine.
Thank you for showing me the world
so that I can write about it!
       —NAOMI ARTEMI

As always, I write for you all, the readers,
and, as always, I thank all those
who helped me write it.
       —DEVIN HUNT

To my parents. Thanks for always
fostering my interests, even when I
said I wanted chickens. They may have
been a lot of hard work, but at least
none of them were like this.
       —CHEYENNE SHAFFER

For Dad, who taught me that history
matters, that you can be kind and tough,
and that being gentle can be
its own form of heroism.
       —KYLE THOMPSON

For my brother.
Cyberpunk will never die!
       —KEEGAN YOUNG

CONTENTS

AS YOU SAY, SO THEY ARE

Kyle Thompson

"And Lot's wife, of course, was told not to look back where all those people and their homes had been. But she did look back, and I love her for that, because it was so human."

Kurt Vonnegut

HLCO Sector 38-1, W-Day+148

The final echoes of shots were still ringing in Elijah's ears. His nose burned with the reek of gunpowder, searing metal, and scorched plastic. His heart pounded with a percussive pell-mell of adrenaline and the ghosts of the artillery rounds that had cleared the way for them into town.

He knew better than to pop his head up in case they'd not destroyed the ambush entirely. Poking your head up when the blinkers knew where you'd taken cover was a good way to hit the ground choking on your own blood. He'd been bait. His job was done. All that was left to do now was to stay hunched behind the burned-out car. Its metal scalded his bicep through his fatigues after being baked in the hot summer sun all day.

"Clear!" Del finally called after moments had drifted off into eternity, "You're good, Jah."

Elijah hated the nickname. He'd always been Elijah. At best, some presumptuous friend or aunt had called him 'El' in an effort to be cute, but never 'Jah.' 'Del' AKA Delilah had introduced it when he'd joined the unit and it had stuck. The early bird gets to pick their nickname he guessed.

Months ago, he might have considered this line of thinking absurd in the middle of a battlefield, but by this point, he was used to the unhelpful way the mind could wander when you were crouched behind a hunk of metal trying not to die.

Elijah rose, shook out his legs and rolled his shoulders before fruitlessly attempting to spit the acrid taste of sweat and propellant out of his mouth. He slipped his finger from his rifle's trigger guard and let the weapon hang limply at his waist to give his aching arms a moment of respite before raising his left hand in a thumbs up above his head.

"I'm good," he called back to the rest of the patrol, "Good shooting."

"Thought the fuckin' blinkers had you, man," Del said.

Elijah jogged back to the mouth of the alley where she stood, still sighting down her rifle at the building down the block, "Nice running."

"Too fast, I guess," he replied with a shrug, pulling his rifle back to a ready position, suddenly conscious of the fact he'd let it rest pointlessly at his side for way too long. The ambush might be done for now, but things could go from calm to holy-fucking-shit-when-will-it-stop in the space between his thundering heart beats.

"What's the play? Pass the barricade and clear the building?"

"Yup. Orders are to clear the town. We're in front, so we take and mark the buildings with shooters in 'em. Echo checks the rest to make sure there aren't any rats laying low," Del replied.

And the day had been going so well until that first round had blown out John's knee. He must've taken more hits as they'd worked to break out of the ambush because he was now slumped between the facade of some blasted out shop front and a rusting postbox. John's chin rested on his chest, his rifle scattered a few feet away. Elijah noted that the mag was already gone from the gun. No time to spare for the dead when the place was still infested, but fresh brass was more valuable than gold.

He opted for his usual, frustrated, "Fuuuuuuuuck," in response.

The blinkers had sprung their ambush from the end of the street, opening fire with rifles and machine guns from what had probably once been a department store, then an office building, then an apartment—one of those buildings that had been around long enough to live many lives. Now, it was a husk.

When towns changed hands as often as this one had in the past few weeks, any and every building that hadn't completely collapsed was pulling double duty as a sometimes-fortress and living space. The squad spent minutes that stretched to infinity carefully leapfrogging each other down the seventy five meters to the three-story brick building.

There were only thirteen of them now and Maria had caught some shrapnel that passed cleanly through her tricep. Nothing was broken, but it was clear that she was in pain. Del left Maria in charge out front, watching the main entrance with four others. She took three around the left and sent Elijah and three others around the right to meet at the back.

The key was speed. If anyone inside the building was still alive, aggression was critical to removing them from the picture without losing more of their own. Even then, it meant leaving as few exits open for escape as possible. On the back corner, Elijah's crew encountered a small fire exit. He left Sarah and Michael behind to hold it, carrying on to meet back up with Del.

Del's group had also found a fire exit and she'd left two to watch it. That left four when they found the back entrance off an old small town commercial parking lot shared by several buildings. The baking asphalt was pocked with the craters of both war and just your classic poor maintenance. A handful of burned-out cars were still scattered about, an old sedan flipped on its roof like some pissed off giant toddler had scattered it when told to pick up their toys.

"No trouble?" Del asked.

"We're good. Let's get this done," Elijah answered.

"Good. Watch corners. Ruben—you're up front. Go."

There was no questioning, just execution. They'd been at this long enough that they worked on instinct. They divided up the rooms and held angles on the stairs and hallways, weaving between each other, swapping positions and roles. They kept their guns up as they entered every room, checking their assigned angle, seeing nothing, leaving and moving on to the next. In peacetime, it would look like a strange modern-art ballet using the whole building as the stage. It was a threatening, angular dance, all pounding boots and clattering polymers punctuated by smacked shoulders marking the time to move on to the next step.

The first two floors passed uneventfully. They found the occasional body in varied states of decomposition.

"Fuckin' blinkers are savages, man," someone muttered when they came across one such corpse, arms ending in ragged stumps and face a mess of shattered bone and muscle. They couldn't even tell what color eyes the guy once had.

Elijah knew that this town had changed hands so much in the past few weeks, there was just as much chance that any given body had been left by their side, but he didn't bother correcting anyone. It didn't matter who killed this guy—the blinkers were monsters who couldn't be tamed. They started this whole mess by coming to this country in the first place. If they'd just stayed out or at the very least shut up and did their work like everyone else, this whole fucking mess wouldn't be necessary.

On the third floor, the tension was threatening to crush all of them. Elijah's heart had finally started to settle as they'd made their way here, but it was back to crashing against his ribs as he climbed the steps. He prayed the damned stairs were even so he wouldn't trip over his own feet while his eyes were peering down his gunsight. At least he was second in line. Hopefully, Simon would trip first over any errant step—then Elijah could just slide into place in front of him and would know to pick up his feet a little more.

Elijah was grateful to finally crest the staircase and flow into the upper hallway. In its many conversions, the top floor must have been divided into a pair of penthouses. Del had split left, meaning she'd lead a group into the penthouse facing the rear of the building. Elijah was looking right, heading towards the apartment the shooters had been in. Mentally, he let out another frustrated, "Fuuuuuck." It was a real wrong place, wrong time kinda day.

There was no time for hesitation though. Hesitating meant slowing down the momentum. It meant more of them might die.

The door to the apartment had long since been pulled from its hinges, probably to add to a barricade somewhere. Elijah passed through it quickly, trusting someone was following in behind him, watching his blind spots. The whole place was open concept—a nightmare of scattered furniture and debris in a space that afforded free sightlines to most of the apartment. Better than the hallway and the doorway, but too many places for blinkers to lurk behind counters and sofas and all the intermingling concrete and drywall dust; too few places for him to seek cover if someone got the jump on him.

He could feel his blood pumping into his trigger finger. He was ready for any sign of movement. Time stretched out so thin, he knew it was bound to snap. Each step felt like it took an age, but he was through the living-room-slash-kitchen in a moment. He checked a closet stacked with empty tins of ammo that reeked like a bathroom and a room stacked with comms equipment and a battery, before he finally entered a blasted out bedroom.

Shell casings rolled and pinged off each other as Elijah crossed the room to check behind what remained of the bed. He stepped over a body at the foot of the bed, snapping a shot into its head as he approached to be certain it didn't sit up and pop him in the back. The stench of propellant and sweat hung in the air.

Ears still ringing from the shot he'd fired, Elijah was forced to shoot again as he rounded the ruined bed frame. A gutshot blinker was behind it, rifle still in hand. The shots were amplified in the confined space. Each blast pounded against Elijah's eardrums. Crimson bloomed on the blinker's chest and right below his left eye.

Elijah paused for a breath just to make sure he was dead before turning on his heel to confirm they'd finished clearing the room.

His ears still buzzed with gunfire, but Elijah could just make out a, "Clear!" from the other side of the room, "We got 'em."

"Clear," he echoed loudly.

"Christ," Simon said from the other side of the room as the tension started to evaporate into the air, "Get a load of this blinker bullshit."

Elijah looked to where Simon was standing, staring at one of the bedroom's interior walls.

"Looks like this idiot went nuts when she got hit."

Unable to see the tableau clearly, Elijah stepped back around the ruined bed and paced up to Simon. In front of him lay a woman on what was once a high-end hardwood floor, her forearm bent awkwardly up the wall, legs bent strangely like she'd just run out of steam and crumpled downward onto them. She was clearly dead, torso and face all coated in blood, but it was impossible to see where she'd been hit and what had done her in. Most likely she just caught a load of shrapnel and bled out when some artery or another was severed.

That was not what had caught Simon's attention though. The woman had daubed a message in her own blood on the bullet-riddled drywall.

"As you say, so they are," Elijah read aloud as he stopped next to Simon, "The fuck does that mean?"

"Who knows, man. Blinkers do crazy shit. That's what happens to your brain when you ain't got the fear of God in you. Fuckers are loons. Who thinks, 'Ah let me write out some cryptic BS in my own blood when I'm hit?' Not me, man. That's for sure."

"How you know she's a blinker? She's got on civvies."

"She was up here with 'em. What else would she be?"

Elijah didn't have an answer for that, not that Simon would've listened to one. He'd waved his hand and wandered away, probably to grab a smoke before they moved back out to trip the next ambush.

He took one last look at the woman, decided Simon must be right, and turned to go find Del and debrief. Being on the knife's edge of death had spiked his adrenaline and the comedown was making him nauseous. He wanted to be done with this place and on to the next before he crashed out completely.

ULFED WZ-115, W-Day+255

"You got him, Chen?" asked Lefty. He said their name more to ensure attention and focus. Observation work was long, quiet, and worst of all, boring. It didn't hurt to wake up your buddy every once in a while.

"Check."

Chen wasn't so much what Lefty would call stocky. Compact was probably a better descriptor. They were certainly short and muscular, but almost improbably, all that brawn was tightly packed and stacked on top of itself. Despite that, Chen looked like they could squeeze into just about any space, no matter how tight.

Lefty supposed that made for a great sniper—they were hard to spot, could get places a lot of other folks couldn't, and were able to lug around a gun that was longer than they were tall without too much trouble.

Lefty was glad the infiltration part of the mission was done. Keeping up with Chen, especially when they could squeeze beneath rubble as if walking through a door, was frustrating at the best of times and painful at the worst. Sitting under cover in a tangle of partly scorched and mostly dead bushes of some old park in what was once a city literally pissing his pants for the next day or two was not Lefty's idea of a great time, but it definitely beat feeling like an overpacked sausage in a rubble casing.

It had taken them about nine hours of stalking to get to the elevated park. The busted-up sign was too splintered to be legible at this point, so Lefty had no idea where they were exactly, but it gave them a near perfect view of the boar HQ. Through his spotter scope he could see into a few of the windows of the shell-hollowed office building. Even better was the primo view of the main entrance. Sure there were concrete barricades, concertainers, makeshift guard houses and other pockets of cover everywhere, but there was a perfect, three to four second gap where anyone that came in or out could be put down, should Chen and he deem it so.

The mission was simple. Watch the place, write down what they saw, and if they got a clean shot on a VIP, take it and exfil, but only if they'd been in place for a full day first. Part intel gathering, and maybe an assassination. Now that they were here, as long as they laid low, the most dangerous bit would be getting back out again.

Truthfully, sneaking around behind Chen was enough of a pain in the ass. Lefty was hoping they didn't spot anyone worthwhile or that the conditions would be too poor to take a shot. If Chen pulled that trigger, getting out would require a lot more speed and could mean a series of fighting and disengaging as the boars tried to pin them in place. Avoiding capture sounded like a fucking nightmare to Lefty—slinking away in the dark sounded a lot more peaceful.

"That's just a captain." Despite the calm quiet in Chen's voice and the fact that he'd just guided them to look at the distant man exiting the building, Lefty jumped, "Chill, man. Stay focused."

"Sorry."

"Infil was clean. Nobody knows we're up here. I set a decoy blind in the building on the corner and we got the motion trips all over the place. We'll know if anyone's around. If they get through all that, the bouncer will definitely give us back the initiative if some boar steps on that."

"I said I was sorry. Just spooked me in the quiet." Lefty tried again.

Chen went quiet again and Lefty wasn't entirely sure if it was some passive-aggressive way to get under his skin or just Chen being Chen. They hadn't even pulled their eyes from their respective scopes for the whole exchange, so it was tough to get a read on Chen's body language.

They spent the entire day that way—calmly muttering out calls to confirm with each other what they'd seen in terse language. Lefty would occasionally look back from his scope to check notes and add to their log. Beyond that, neither of them moved a muscle for hours on end.

Lefty's back was screaming as night started to fall and with the gloom came a delicate fall drizzle that soaked them through despite the cover of the bushes.

Mist. Visibility: Fuck all. he scribbled into the log in the last of the dying light.

"It's just shapes now," Chen said, "Can see 'em moving, but can't even tell an APC from a technical. Shit."

"Yup," Lefty sighed, "Wanna rest first or should I?"

"I'm good. You go."

Lefty shook his head and smirked as he pulled back from the spotter scope and blinked to reset his vision (and attempt to stave off the headache that had settled behind his right eye), "Yeah, for sure. I'll just head to the penthouse suite and get a tight eight. Maybe I'll get room service."

"Order me some carbonara, would ya?" Chen asked flatly.

"No problem."

Lefty lowered his forehead onto the soft weight that helped anchor the spotter scope.

"Swap you in four."

"Check. Sleep tight, sweetheart."

Lefty grinned into the dirt at the old bit, "Night, honey."

* * *

The pre-dawn glow was just staining the horizon a pale yellow. Chen had raised their head about twenty minutes earlier and resumed their shooting posture like they'd never gone to sleep in the first place.

The rain had finally drifted off sometime in the middle of the night. While he was freezing cold, he was grateful it had drenched them so thoroughly. Lefty's back no longer ached since most of his muscles had gone numb from the chill. It also spread out the stench of sweat and urine, masking them just that much more if anyone wandered too close.

"Fuck," Lefty sighed when he spotted the rank insignia on the woman's shoulder as she entered the HQ, "General. Two stars. Just going in."

"Scanning," Chen paused for a breath. They'd been surveying the surrounds, watching for guards, counter snipers, and other problems while Lefty watched the door. "Check. Got 'em. Pony-tail. Glasses. Dark hair?"

"Check. She's in."

"We bag that little piggy when she comes back out."

"It's never fuckin' easy," Lefty muttered as he glanced down and logged the general's arrival amidst a crew of lower-ranking officers.

Chen maintained their site down the scope, "Hey. War doesn't end until we put down enough boars."

It was a gentle scolding, issued in Chen's clipped, professional voice. Somehow, that got under Lefty's skin more. Chen was right—this was a juicy target, but would it really be too much to ask to not have to get out of this blasted hell hole with a bunch of shooters hunting for them?

"Check," was all Lefty could muster.

"Resuming scanning. Let me know as soon as you got move-ment on the door," Chen said, brushing past the tension like nothing happened, which only pissed Lefty off more.

He knew it was just fatigue setting in. Laying still watching people come and go from a building for a full day would get on anyone's nerves. Lefty dropped his mind into checking their range and other shot details, knowing full well the general was probably going to be inside most of the day handling briefings and the other mundane details of the military machine. It was funny to Lefty that the most effort went into killing the ones with the most boring jobs.

The numbers refocused his mind and he let the frustration slip away. He kept updating Chen on windage and any movement over the next several hours. Occasionally, Chen would give details on vehicles and troop counts as they scanned around the target building.

Lefty could no longer let his eye drift from the spotter scope, so he did his best to make notes blind, without fully taking his focus off that damned door. It had started to feel like it was taunting him. It would open occasionally and some NCO or runner would step out briskly and half jog, half walk to carry out whatever order they'd been given.

Finally, it swung open and a small group of low ranking commissioned officers stepped out, clearly solidifying and confirming orders.

"Looks like the meetings are over. You're up."

"Check. Contact on door," Chen answered, followed immediately by the light click of the rifle's safety coming off.

Shhhhnk, clack, shhhhnk, chunk.

Chen had chambered a round and was ready to fire. The window for the shot was tight. They'd agreed to start the shooting process so Chen could fire as any target was coming out the door. They would have to start confirming details using the boars walking out of the building first.

"Check mill."

"One point one three," Chen said, already sinking into deep breathing, readying for the shot.

"Check level," Lefty took a quick look at his ballistic calculator, confirming he'd landed on the same mill earlier while watching personnel leave the building throughout the day, "Holdover. Eight point six."

Chen kept their breathing slow and steady. Thirty seconds sped by. The door swung open again and out walked the general accompanied by some other toady. Lefty gave the call as soon as she was clear in his scope, "Target. Woman. Left."

"Ready."

As soon as the sound of the 'r' was clearing Chen's lips, Lefty was checking windage for the final shot, "Right. Point five."

CRACK!

The rifle shot rang in Lefty's ears. A second later, there was a spray of atomized blood from the general, followed by a thick red spurt as her heart pumped her life away out of the new hole in her throat. She took an awkward step as if she'd suddenly gotten extremely drunk, before toppling backwards and slumping against the door she'd just finished walking through.

"Target down."

There was no further chatter. No celebration. There was no need for conversation. The mission accomplished, all that was left was to bug out as quickly as possible. Chen and Lefty scooted back further into the bush, collapsing gear as they went. The cleanup didn't have to be perfect. They wouldn't be coming back.

Lefty went first, carefully skirting the bouncer they'd left to cover their rear. With any luck, some dumb boar would trip it and they'd bag a second without any extra work. It'd be a nobody, but a dead boar was a dead boar.

Chen was just crawling out of the brush when Lefty heard a noise that made his stomach drop. A half dozen distant thumps and a moment later, a faint whistling.

"Stay down! Incoming!" Lefty was hardly aware that the voice was his.

The mortars thudded down one right after the other, walking across the park. Lefty felt the earth jump beneath him with each impact. When it was over, his ears still ringing, he jumped up and glanced towards where Chen had been. There was nothing there but a small crater.

"Fuck!" Lefty shouted, but couldn't hear his own voice. Chen was gone.

The damned boars had a ballistic locator. The mortar squad behind the HQ were a skilled bunch. Their shells had come in fast and accurate.

There was no time to wait around. A QRF would be on him in minutes, if that. And he wouldn't put it past the mortar teams to drop more hate directly on his head.

Lefty turned to run.

Twenty feet in front of him stood Chen. Alive. Unharmed. For the first time since they'd been paired up, Chen's normally stoic face was a twisted comedy mask of confusion and terror. But that wasn't the strangest part—no. Chen's eyes were cataract white—their irises and pupils gone completely as if some artist had suddenly erased them.

Lefty charged forward, grabbed Chen's shoulder, spun them around, and pushed them onward. One second, Chen was in his grasp, the next, they were thirty feet along their escape route, already across the street.

It wasn't possible. Lefty almost tripped following Chen, expecting to still be holding their shoulder. His brain strained to catch up.

Chen stopped, looked at Lefty, all sense of composure gone, and shouted. Lefty could just hear it over the ringing in his ears.

"WHAT'S HAPPENING TO ME?"

HLCO Sector 1-2, W+1193

"Blinkers only exist to destroy. Even an unarmed blinker is a threat. Do not show them mercy. Do not hesitate. If you want to survive, if you want to stop the greatest threat humanity has ever faced from reaching your doorstep, you will kill."

Lilith hated that she'd been pigeonholed. You get a pierced lung and lose most of your dominant arm and you get relegated out of your combat role. Sure, she couldn't run as far or as fast now, but the simple titanium and plastic prosthesis seemed like an asset to her. She could take a hit like few others could. It wasn't like she'd risk bleeding out if she lost the arm again.

She felt like a waste of space and effort—a charity case given a training role because "she really knew what the blinkers were like."

They'd told her she'd already given enough of her body on the front lines. Her people needed no more blood from her. These were nothing but coddling words meant to ease her suffering. But she knew the truth.

She'd been sidelined because she was bad for morale on the battlefield. They needed young men and women who would heedlessly run into danger, convinced they were invincible. A wartime cripple would only remind them that they could, in fact, be horribly maimed or even killed at the hands of the blinkers they were expected to run towards.

After a pause to let the speech sink in—or maybe just for dramatic effect, she wasn't sure anymore—she carried on, "The only thing the blinkers understand is violence. Never assume you are safe when you reach the front. Blinkers are like roaches: you don't always see them, but they're there. They appear out of thin air when they sense easy pickings, so do not make yourself a target! Expect no mercy, and give none in return."

Unless you want to look like me . . .

Command had found a place where her unasked-for body renovation was an asset when they'd stuck her here, hundreds of miles from any hope of paying back her wounds in kind. Apparently, seeing her prosthetic and hearing her now-wheezing voice helped to punctuate the graduation speech she was expected to give after eight intensive weeks of yelling at versions of herself from two years past to move faster, push farther, and fight harder.

That was all well and good, but she still felt like the whole "blinkers are vicious killers who come from nowhere that cannot imagine an evil too cruel for their liking" schtick was perhaps a bit superfluous after The Change. Unleashing a targeted but seemingly virulent bioweapon against your enemy tended to pretty well cement your place among history's biggest assholes.

As if the throbbing non-arm and the wheezing lung weren't enough, Lilith's jaw ached constantly thanks to the upper and lower canines that had grown overnight and pressed past her lips. She was still unused to her sudden bulk. She was muscular with a body hardened by years of military work, but her shoulders had broadened. The docs studying The Change claimed that those infected had a higher bone density, particularly in the skull. How the blinkers had seemingly limited the impact of the weapon to just Lilith's side was a mystery to everyone. But The Change's purpose was an even bigger mystery.

Had the blinkers made a mistake? How was The Change supposed to have worked? Lilith felt monstrous, but conjecture and science alike seemed to agree—when it came to fighting blinkers, The Change was all upside. Better endurance, a thicker skin, a harder head, and knives in your mouth certainly made one feel like an instrument of warfare.

Aching scars and being used as a prop aside, she could not deny a swelling of pride at the classroom in front of her. Fifty hulking bodies stood at ease, freshly graduated from BT, each of them looking like they could take four or five people in a fist fight. Fifty faces with angry, jutting teeth that could tear out throats and eyes full of murder.

They were ready and Goddammit, she felt certain this was the class that would put an end to the blinkers once and for all.

ULFED Homefront, W+1344

"How are you feeling today?"

"You know I hate that question, Doc. Why can't you just start with 'What's up' like a normal person?"

"Because. If you won't engage with your feelings, you won't give yourself space to heal, and if I don't think you're doing better,

I can't greenlight you. You know that. So are you going to answer the question or not?"

"Probably not."

. . .

. . .

"Alright. Let's come back to that one. What about symptoms? Any night terrors still? Flashbacks?"

"Can't have night terrors if you don't sleep, right?"

"Why aren't you sleeping?"

"Is anyone sleeping anymore? Out of nowhere, we all start teleporting all over the place. Our eyes change. The real doctors say there's more shit going on with us they can't explain. I can do literal magic, and you're wondering why I can't sleep."

. . .

"Two weeks ago, we all start growing these crazy things out of our foreheads. I can *feel* the air in here. Every shift. Every muscle twitch. I can feel that. Can you?"

"Yes."

"Well maybe that's why I can't sleep. How are *you* sleeping, Doc? Can you tell me that? You getting a solid eight every night?"

"No. I'm not."

. . .

. . .

"And how does that make you feel, then, Doc?"

"Tired. Short on patience. But I'm happy to acknowledge that. It allows me to be here for the people who need me. To make sure we keep warriors like yourself in the fight."

. . .

. . .

. . .

. . .

"I don't like when you do that."

"What's that?"

"Say smart shit and then sit there all self-assured. Like you know everything. Like you've got people figured out. Like I'm just predictable."

"Are you not predictable?"

"I guess you'd know, wouldn't you?"

. . .

. . .

"Think of it like your job then. You're highly trained. Recon. You go out and get to places that would be too dangerous for larger teams. You gather information. You strike out at weaknesses. You avoid danger that those without your skills can't, so that you can get closer to the enemy, right?"

"The enemy? You mean, the boars."

"If that's the term you prefer."

"Fine. Yes."

"How do you do what you do so well?"

"What do you mean?"

"Is the battlespace not somewhat predictable? Have you not learned to read it? You speak the language of war—you see the patterns around you, and interpret them to keep you safe. To reach your goals. You understand your job completely because it is what allows you to keep doing your job."

"Okay."

"Yes or no?"

"Yes."

"It is the same for me. People aren't entirely predictable. But there are patterns. Those patterns help me to understand my patients better so that I can help them."

. . .

. . .

"You're not a real doctor."

"I'm not here to debate that. I'm here to help you. Your command says that if you want back to the front, I have to do that. It's up to you whether you let me do that or not."

. . .

. . .

"Fine."

. . .

. . .

"Let's start again then. How are you feeling?"

. . .

. . .

"Like a failure."

"Why's that?"

"Because I failed, I guess. I'm still failing."

"Failing how?"

"I can't just be better. Look at me. I don't know what's wrong with my eyes . . . Why they look the way they do . . . I can't see color like I used to . . . I'm not sure I'm seeing like I used to at all. But all that detail was just confusing, I realize now. I understand this room completely. I feel it. I feel every piece of furniture. I feel you sitting over there in that stupid plastic chair. I know everything that's happening in here. I know that your right knee is bouncing and it's driving me up the wall. I know what you're writing just by the scratch of your pen and the way your arm moves. The way it pushes the atmosphere around it."

. . .

"It's raining. There are no windows in here. We're in the middle of a concrete box, pretty deep underground. It was sunny when I came in. How can I know that it's raining right now? You know what I mean, Doc?"

"We've all mutated."

"So?"

"So, yes."

"What has happened to us? I have three inexplicable lumps on my forehead! And look at this. Are you ready? That's right, I'm over here now."

"I know. We can all do that now."

"But why?"

"Does it matter? Is that not a useful ability in your work?"

"Sure. But have you seen a boar lately?"

"No, but I've been briefed on what's out there."

"They're fucking nightmares, Doc. Remember what we all used to look like? Two arms, two legs, two eyes, all that shit? Sure we could be fit, but there was kinda a limit right?"

"I'm aware."

"Take the whole Mr. Universe thing and double it. Everything is just bigger. I don't even know how they get around. And they've got fangs or tusks or something now. You let one get close, they'll just eat you. They're faster than you'd think. They're angry all the time. Hell, I saw one get shot in the head *and shake that shit off.* Are you following me, Doc?"

. . .

"So yeah. Maybe we've mutated and it worked out for us. Survival of the fittest. I know the real doctors don't know shit about what's going on. Telling us it can't be mutation. Whatever. But whatever we got, the boars got just as good. Maybe better. I'm telling you. Picture the biggest, most savage, violent creature you can. Now try to make it worse and you might finally be close to what we're really facing out there. So maybe that's why despite, our new super powers, I still feel a little behind the curve."

"But that's not you failing. We're all in the same boat. Aren't we? So what have you, specifically, failed at?"

"This. All of this. War. I'm supposed to be out there killing those fuckers, but I can't get my shit straight. Instead, I'm in here. Safe. Talking to you. Everyone I care about is out there doing their jobs or already dead, and I'm in here with you. You don't call that mission failure, then what the hell is it, Doc?"

. . .

. . .

"It's being human, Florence."

"I'm not sure any of us are anymore, Doc."

HLCO Sector 71-5, W+5205

Something made his arm hair stand on end and he knew to trust his instincts. He paused and made a fist.

Gabriel found himself hoping that the new squad was able to track his hand signals. The Change had forced them away from speaking as their jaws had distended and they began to lose all ability to even slur language. In war, when stealth was often useful, if not a matter of survival, signaling your mates with your hands had long been practiced.

But, when your very physiology seemed to be painfully and uncontrollably shifting thanks to your enemy's war crimes, communication amongst your own kind had to change with it. And when several of your fingers fused together over the course of the past few years, your old hand signals stopped working or got muddled together. It led to each squad organically evolving their own adjusted Handspeak to compensate.

Gabriel held his trigger hand by his waist, both meaty fingers pressed tightly together, thumb extended outward. *Get low. Stay quiet.*

The squad seemed to get the message. Hulking shoulders dipped as everyone bent their already curving spines further and settled back onto their haunches.

They were here, fumbling through the dark of these old bombed-out sewers, hoping to surprise a blinker headquarters. The goal was to gather all the intel and equipment they could find, and bomb the rest.

Gabriel cursed the blinkers for their newfound love of dark spaces and night time. It meant even daytime pushes like this were usually done in pitch black environments. His amplified sense of smell was not doing him any favors here. Decades of human effluent and the sick scent of years of war dead assaulted his senses. He wasn't sure if he could even pick out the reek of a live blinker from a dead one.

And that could be the fatal flaw of this whole mission. Blinkers were best caught off-guard. Otherwise, things tended to get complicated with their uncanny ability to vanish and reappear elsewhere. Gabriel remembered that his first drill instructor had told him that the enemy were called blinkers due to how cowardly they were. They were weak and would flinch at the first sign of strength. The name seemed to suit them better now.

As they crouched in the dark, everyone's breath had gone shallower. They were all doing what he was—listening carefully. Quietly sniffing the air. Looking for any sign of trouble in the deep black of the old tunnel.

There was the faint sound of conversation somewhere up ahead! The smell might be masking the blinkers, but his sensitive hearing could still catch them. He quietly shifted forward a few steps and the squad followed, their footsteps soft, but distinctly spattering in the muck that drenched this whole Godforsaken place.

He squinted through the noise of the NVGs that were crudely strapped to his face—the damned helmets didn't fit anymore, so they'd improvised a rig that didn't rely on the helmet mount— looking for any sign of where the blinkers might be. There it was. A dark offshoot tunnel, opening out of the grimy darkness to the right. He wasn't certain if this was the HQ they were looking for, but the blinkers were here. He might not recognize himself anymore, but at least it was easy to tell friend from foe when your side couldn't really speak.

Gabriel paused again and made a fist with his offhand and gently tapped it to his ear.

Hearing protection.

Were his ears slightly pointed now? He couldn't remember that. He'd worry about that later. Right now he had a job to do.

Command had given them heavy duty hearing protection for

this mission. They didn't give the particulars, but several soldiers had gone fully deaf after a singular battle. More had reported severe anxiety and disorientation. Gabriel was pretty sure the latter was just part of being in a gunfight, but he wasn't going to argue if it meant his ears wouldn't be ringing when this was over.

He slid the headphones over his ears. All noise stopped. He knew he hadn't gone deaf because he could still hear the muffled sound of his own movement, but the ambient whoosh of stagnant air through the tunnels disappeared.

He reshouldered his rifle and made a fist, but held his index/middle finger out, curved, almost like a question mark.

Ready?

A moment later came the gentle squeeze of his shoulder from behind.

Ready.

Gabriel rose from his crouched stance and quickly strode to the dark opening of the offshoot tunnel. He rounded the corner and pushed forward, knowing that to stand in the opening would make him an easy target. He'd hoped the passage would open into a wider room, but no such luck—it was just another damn tunnel.

Barely aware of how much noise he was making with the headphones, he held his breath to keep from letting out an exasperated grunt. He just did what he'd trained to do and kept moving forward, enlarged finger on the trigger. Like the NVGs, they'd had to modify their kit as they'd undergone The Change. The quartermaster had cut out the trigger guard on all their weapons to accommodate the fused digits.

After following the curve of the tunnel for thirty or forty feet, Gabriel could see that it was opening up to some other chamber just in front of him. The way the IR torch was devoured by the sudden darkness unnerved him, but he kept pushing forward.

Passing through the exit passage of the tunnel briefly gave him the sensation of untethering from reality, but he was quickly grounded when he turned right and the IR torch showed him a small encampment constructed in what must've once been some kind of flow control room. A few rows of cots were lined up in one corner in front of him. Crates of equipment were stacked carefully around them. It looked like the timing had worked out—the blinkers had taken mostly to nighttime operations and it looked like the majority of them were asleep. Despite the darkness all around, Gabriel knew it was nearly noon.

He scanned for movement. Sleeping blinkers could be dealt with after anyone on guard duty was down.

There! A tall man stepped around some makeshift wall, saying something to . . . someone. Gabriel wasn't sure if the words were directed at him, or just the continuation of the conversation he'd heard before he'd donned the hearing protection. His rifle rammed against his shoulder and his NVGs flared slightly with the light of the shot. He followed the first with several more, tracing a line downwards toward the ground as the man fell, hitting him several more times.

The bark of the rifle was so faint through the hearing protection were it not for the recoil punching him in the shoulder, Gabriel was pretty sure he could sleep through what must in reality be a pounding cacophony. The sleeping blinkers were certainly going to be scrambling to arm themselves now.

But all that Gabriel heard was a faint *wumpf wumpf wumpf.*

A stream of tracers split the air from those who'd followed

him into the room. It took him a few moments to realize that he was still shooting, too. Instinct had taken over and he was ruthlessly firing into the beds of groggy blinkers trying to gain their feet. Understanding what he was doing did nothing to stop him. If anything, he squeezed the trigger faster, snapping the barrel of his rifle from target-to-target.

Gabriel stormed onward, moving to get a view of where the first target had emerged. Passing behind the ramshackle wall, he found a blinker, strange irisless eyes positively glowing in his infrared light. The man was sitting, pushed back up against a makeshift counter. He held his hands up, palms forward.

Instinct flared again before Gabriel had even fully recognized that there was a blinker in front of him. His rifle bucked and the man was gone. Gabriel was already spinning. The man was almost immediately behind him, clearly intending to cause the rest of the squad to hesitate so they didn't shoot their own. Gabriel smashed his rifle butt into the back of the blinker's head, let go of the grip, and pulled the man towards him by the hair.

He roared and sank his enlarged canines into the blinker's exposed throat. Hot blood pumped into Gabriel's mouth as he thrashed his head back and forth. He was conscious of the fact that the blinker was beating his fists into his head, but the punches didn't hurt at all. Gabriel didn't stop working his jaw until the blinker quit moving.

ULFED TAC Network, W+5207

To: All Field Commanders
From: Central Command
Subject: General Order 492

We have received reports of a brutal offensive on a field aid station. Wounded personnel and field medics were all executed with no survivors and no prisoners taken.

Consider the following amended standing orders that remain in effect until superseded by a future General Order. These RoE changes are effective immediately and supersede all current standing RoE orders.

a. Aid stations are to be fortified and all medical personnel are to be properly armed. Guards should be posted at all possible means of ingress.

b. Given the boars' savage and flagrant inhumane behavior, consider all boar targets valid for prosecution without quarter, hesitation, or warning. Terminate with extreme prejudice.

c. Prisoners are not to be taken as surrender cannot be trusted. This includes wounded enemy boars. They have proven resilient, even when grievously injured. Refer to Operating Procedure 6801.c for updated best practices for properly terminating boar soldiery.

General Marchesi
Acting Commander-in-Chief

No Official Designations Remain, W+????

The world is now a quiet place of grays and browns. A rusty sunset strains through clouds of ash and smoke. Strange mounds of concrete and metal slowly decay and go back to the dirt, broken and buried by wind, fire, and rain.

No goldenrod yellow or halogen white street lamps struggle as the darkness begins to claim the planet once again. They have long since been toppled or broken, destroyed by the cold, unfeeling machinery of war. It doesn't matter. There are no longer legs striding down wide boulevards, marching towards the latest fashion trends. There are no longer arms looking to embrace lovers or friends or family members they'd not held in far too long.

There are no longer fingers to pull triggers or press buttons to drop bombs.

No. This is a world where the night is no longer even lit by fire. It is a fearful place of rending claws and ripping teeth—a hungry world where life is but a currency to be stolen from others and hoarded greedily.

In the dimming sunlight, two such monsters struggle in this very paradigm. Standing on what was once an impeccable hardwood floor that now is more splinters and mold than wood, a hulking mass of muscle and fat, its maw filled with massive incisors and other smaller teeth shaped for cutting and tearing, heaves as it pants and readies itself for yet another bout for survival. The beast lets out a guttural roar as it charges again, pounding over pancaked ruins towards another creature.

This other monster is thin and lanky, six appendages tipped with two strange segmented and barged digits. Its body is slick and chitinous, the fading orange of the sun glinting off black-brown armor. The thing's face is a horror, twitching antennae stretching from its forehead, with three strange black orbs resting just below them. Two milky white eyes run like spilled egg yolks around the sides of its cranium. It has no ears and no nose, but a ghastly cartoonish mouth rests at the bottom edge of its face, looking like some long-gone cartoonish theater mask.

A boar and a blinker, still trying to settle a debate that has spanned generations: which of them is predator and which of them is prey.

Just as the boar is about to reach the blinker and gore it on its massive lower jaw, the blinker suddenly disappears. It reappears behind and above the boar, falling onto the thing's back. The boar is clearly prepared for this, dropping to its belly and rolling, throwing its strange three-fingered limbs wide to catch its foe, determination glinting in its humanoid blue eyes.

Not to be outdone, the blinker drives its four forward arms towards the boar as gravity does its work, pulling the two together in a deadly embrace. The barbed digits of the blinker work just like the cruel tips of arrows, weapons that have not seen use in centuries, as they pierce the boar's throat and chest and guts.

But with all its might, the boar closes its hulking arms around the blinker and crushes it to itself. The boar dips its head on instinct as the blinker crashes in, ramming two of its incisors into the sensitive jelly of its enemy's eyes.

Both monsters briefly wail and buck, appendages a confused mess of tangled flesh and chitin. Their torsos thrust against each other a few times before they both collapse, their species' eternal battle still without a decisive answer as the sun finally drops below the horizon.

Blood from both combatants mixes and pools at the base of a strange monument to what came before them: a pockmarked and moldering bit of wall daubed messily in some black-red substance that has stood the test of time. It says, in characters none living remembers how to read . . .

AS YOU SAY, SO THEY ARE

SAM AND THE NIGHT SHIFT

DEVIN HUNT

There was always work for someone who could be anyone. Boss? Check. Ex girlfriend? Check. Neighbor? Check. Black? White? Short? Tall? All check. Step sister? Way more often than expected as of late, but quadruple check.

This was something Sam could do. The 'something' *only* Sam could do. An art so ancient and arcane that it had been all but forgotten.

Men usually came to Sam expecting a cheap imitation, a bit of makeup, platform shoes, stuffed shirts, all made real enough by dim lighting, *a lot* of wishful thinking and blinding lust. But what Sam offered was so much more.

Each request included a picture, brief notes on the person in the photograph, and often instructions. Sam donned a dress like the one the client had asked for: plunging neckline, slit up to the hip, in an alluring scarlet. They touched up their face and by the time they heard him arrive in the foyer, chatting with their receptionist, Kiera (not her real name, but that was for the best in this line of work), Sam was ready for their appointment.

The finished outfit reminded them a little of Jessica Rabbit, but it blew him away, Sam could tell. He didn't say so, but he showed it by how quickly he crossed the room, how he couldn't contain his shuddering groan as he finished, how he smiled—almost embarrassed—as he dragged out his leaving.

As the sun rose, Sam and Kiera made their final costume change: back into street clothes. Kiera waved goodbye, and Sam walked home as morning bloomed into day. Finally alone, *au natural* in their bed, they slept until evening.

***

Sam awoke before their alarm, stood up and stretched—an action that had unnerved the few people who had ever witnessed it. Their limbs popped and cracked, briefly extending a foot or so longer than could be conventionally understood as a normal human length. They luxuriated in their little bedroom, the secret sanctum of their home where they could be themselves, surrounded by the hanging Zulu masks, Peruvian blankets, even a dented kabuto helmet they had worn into battle, once upon a time—souvenirs from their many lives.

Thankfully, death and pain were long behind them now. The many facets of pleasure and ease appealed far more than killing and destruction, these days.

The autumn sun was setting, which meant it was time to start their workday. Sam adopted the androgynous face they'd sculpted for their driver's license and left home for the 'office', checking the PO box that they kept on the way to work. Given the strange tokens of appreciation that satisfied customers sometimes sent, it was best that mail didn't arrive directly at their house.

Sam ducked out of sight and down a discreet staircase to the basement apartment they rented. It wasn't much on the outside, but, like Sam, it was the inside that counted. The inside was all crimson silks and plush, cushioned chairs. Kiera was already there, tidying up her desk, one Sam had carved themselves late in the 18th century.

Sam locked the door behind them, and the two headed into the expansive changing room they shared to prepare. Gorgeous and with a head for numbers, Kiera was the best receptionist Sam could have asked for, but, most importantly, she put clients at ease. She had almost asked to work a few of them once or twice, Sam could tell.

Kiera pulled a top from her bag to complete her alluring ensemble for the evening. Finished, she did a twirl for Sam to assess.

Sam stroked their chin. "Hmm . . . it's missing something"

Kiera struck a comedic grimace at her boss's reluctance to pass approval over her clearly perfect outfit. Sam smiled. "There! That face is just what it needed!"

Kiera laughed as she handed Sam the tablet with the night's schedule and all the people Sam would become.

Tonight held particular promise: the roster listed a few repeat clients who Sam genuinely liked. The uptown bartender had been Sam's client a few times already, and they could slip into the now-familiar shape of his beautiful—though married—coworker easily, like slipping feet into well-loved shoes.

The more they *wore* the person, the more they *were* the person.

Each time they smoothed their eye sockets into her precise shape, sculpted their lips just so, they understood the woman better and better, and understood a little more why the man loved her so much.

They adjusted their posture, cracked their neck, and opened the door.

***

The night passed as Sam had expected, shape after shape.

The last image was a scan of an old photograph: a young Japanese girl. Sam always refused clients who asked for young girls; those kinds of men tended to talk to each other, and that wasn't a reputation Sam wanted. However, as Sam scanned the instructions, they decided to break their normal rule, just this once. What was Sam if not flexible?

Sam cleansed themselves of their last client's scent as they studied the photograph carefully, like a portrait painter, and prepared their blank form for shaping. Sam worked slowly and gently with their hands, compressing their adult body into the size and height of the girl in the picture. Sam thumbed in the young girl's dimples delicately, opening and closing the mouth and smiling to make sure they perfectly matched the dimples in the picture. Next, Sam massaged the jaw and throat, dusting off the cobwebs of an old East Okinawan accent as they dressed. The voice was usually the hardest part, but after centuries and a sea of blood, Sam would never forget the subtleties of how that accent was done, and it completed the young girl nicely.

Sam was reading a book on the chaise lounge, kicking feet which no longer reached the floor, when they heard the drag of shoes and the knocking of a cane with every other step. Their heightened senses picked out the degraded fatty acids that signaled a gentleman of failing health and *extremely* advanced age.

When a gentle knock sounded from the door, Sam rose and opened it, bowing deeply.

The man stilled at the sight of her, only a desperate "Oh," escaping his throat before it clenched shut. His cane fell, ignored, as he tried and failed again to speak, reaching out with trembling hands. Sam stepped close, ensuring he didn't fall, offering him the girl's delicate little arm, leading him to sit on the bed and coming to rest beside him.

His eyes darted across the girl, taking Sam in. A shaking hand reached out to stroke her cheek, flinching away at the feel of Sam's skin.

He swallowed hard and managed to say, "Can you ever forgive me?"

He turned his hands up so Sam could see them. He had been horribly burned once, and old, rippling scars covered both palms, down to the tips of his fingers.

"Of course, *Ojichan*."

"I couldn't . . . the smoke . . . I couldn't lift it."

"You were strong to try."

"I tried, I . . . I wasn't . . ." His fragile, failing body shudders with the first sob of the night. It wouldn't be the last.

"You are only one man," Sam said as they folded their tiny fingers around his, as much to offer comfort as to feel the whorls and irregularities of the texture: a challenging, non-repeating pattern they would attempt to replicate later.

He wept—bitter, explosive, ugly and beautiful. He wept until he was empty. It was the first time he'd ever cried for his granddaughter, Sam could tell. Sometimes removing pain was as good for a person as giving pleasure.

He squeezed the soft little hands with his scarred ones and sighed, a sigh decades in coming, deep and final.

Sam was glad to have brought him peace as his time came to an end.

AGGRESSIVE MIMICRY

Naomi Artemi

On the busiest corner of Boulevard Barbès and Place du Château-Rouge, beside the entrance to the sketchiest metro stop in all of Paris, stands a public toilet so foul that even the crackheads won't smoke up in there, the prostitutes won't blow in there, and the runaways won't shelter from a cold and dreary rain in there, either.

Inside, it reeks of ammonia and fermented asparagus. Sometimes a drunk will stumble in at night to urinate until, inevitably, he will feel a wet heat soaking his shoes and creeping up his socks. Only then will he realize that he is standing in a box painted completely black, with no toilet, no sink, and no clearly marked exit. At this point, he will feel that he should evacuate more than his bladder, careful never to get drunk on that same corner again.

The only people who willingly enter to find relief therein are the ones you would never expect: stockbroker wearing a tailored suit with buttonholes all stitched at a 45-degree slant, socialite type in head-to-toe designer, Chinese tourist with a Canon EOS-1D X Mark III around his neck.

If you were, say, a homeless man watching from across the street in your flop of soggy cardboard, you would see these unlikely bathroom-goers stop at the door with something suspiciously shitesque smeared on the handle, take a furtive glance out the corner of each eye, and slip inside. Then you would try to tell passersby, but they would only think you unhinged and unmedicated. And, though that may be true, it wouldn't make you any less right.

For these patrons of the toilette publique are not bothered by the stench of hundreds of drunk pissings because they are not bothered by the stench of anything. Because they cannot smell. Because their noses are not real. Their noses, their faces, their bodies, from the double chins to the toenails that really need a trim. It all takes effort to hold these distinct shapes, especially in a city where so many others tempt. A few times a day, it just becomes too much to maintain, and these imitators extraordinaire must find relief in the complete dark of the foul, coffin-like, black box and let their façade blur into featureless bliss.

Lis was one such mimicker, or 'freeformer,' as their kind thought themselves. How Lis knew this public toilet would be a place of respite was a matter of animalistic instinct—same way a clownfish knows a sea anemone as a safe haven. And so, they walked up to the shit-smeared door in their pink tweed, Chanel sneaker-boots and quickly glanced in each direction.

It was noontime on an unseasonably scorching September Monday, and the lunch hustle was full bustle. A voluptuous woman dragging a granny trolly behind her, bounced and jiggled and rattled past. Another in a mustard-yellow headwrap fussed over the child on her hip. Her dusty red flip-flops smacked the sidewalk and slapped back at calloused heels. A pair of Adidas slides walked in the other direction. The human male in them wore black jeans and a black Calvin Klein shirt, despite the heat. His deep brown, bald head shone in the bright sun like the gilded dome of Napoleon's tomb.

It was all too much.

No one seemed to notice Lis loitering by the toilet (there was a homeless human across the street, but he didn't count). Lis slid inside.

They let their brown skin drain of color. Their head of heavy burgundy braids melt. Their slender shape beneath the lavender denim romper and logo-patterned shoulder bag soften. Relief! A feeling that was not unlike releasing a very full bladder.

Suddenly, the black box cracked open.

"Occupied!" Lis shrieked as they hastily pulled their shape back on.

"Maybe lock the door next time," suggested the man standing on the other side of it. He had a gut that tested his shirt buttons and a bristly mustache that made Lis' upper lip itch to imitate.

He held out his hand like he wanted to shake, but then— Lis noticed that the man's pinky nail had turned a lavender that matched their own mimicked nails. One of their kind! For humans, imitation may be the sincerest form of flattery, but for a freeformer, it is the surest way to stay off a fellow hunter's menu.

Lis held out their own hand, letting their pinky copy one of his dirt-caked nails. At this, he shook it.

"Too bad," the other freeformer said in their language, which was spoken with thought and not the slab of tongue, wet in their approximation of a mouth with its abundance of spit-slick teeth. "I'm looking for lunch."

A joke? Lis smiled out of politeness.

"Wait a moment?" the mustached freeformer asked, nodding to the lavatory that Lis had only just vacated.

Lis wished they'd had more of a chance to relax in there themselves, but in Freespeak, they answered, "Of course."

"Be just a jiffy." He closed the door.

Lis stood outside, earning a look or two from passing pedestrians, but more for taking up sidewalk real estate than proximity to the repugnant public toilet. To avoid the stares of strangers, Lis looked up. Classic Parisian buildings with balconied windows bordered the boulevard, all tan stone, all veneered with soot. Most had awnings of varying degree of tattiness. Onto one was bolted a neon green plus sign. It was remarkable how much more Lis could see as a bipedal.

"Ah, much better," said the freeformer as he exited. "So?"

He was obviously waiting for Lis to reply somehow, but they weren't sure what they were meant to say.

"You new to this territory?" he prompted.

"I'm new to being human, actually."

"Oh! Welcome to humanhood. What species you coming from? Chimp? Orangutan? *Waah Ah Ah*, as the Bonobos say?" He chuckled at his own cleverness and his over-inflated balloon of a belly bounced, looking like it was about to pop, along with a few shirt buttons.

"Dog."

"Dog to human?! Impatient, aren't we?" the freeformer scoffed. Then, not waiting for an answer, asked, "Which way you headed?"

"I'm not sure." Lis only knew they wanted to get off the crowded street. Retreating back inside to regroup seemed the best course of action. Before venturing out, they'd taken a piece of mail with them from the apartment where their prey had lived. Lis showed the addressed envelope to the other freeformer.

Rokhaya Kebe
12 Rue Léon
75018 Paris
France

The freeformer nodded his human head to the left, and they started to walk together down the busy boulevard.

Mania rose from the pavement like heat waves. People hurrying past carrying packages. Pushing strollers. Weaving through the crowd on bicycles, shopping bags swinging from the handlebars and whacking those on foot whose feet did not move them out of the way fast enough. More plastic bags—blue bags, black bags, red and white striped bags—congregated against the base of every street sign and cast-iron bollard.

"But I get it, I get it," the freeformer continued, picking their conversation back up as he navigated around one such congregation of rubbish. "Humans are certainly intriguing. They fill you up a heck of a lot longer, and their last thoughts are much juicer, too."

"I noticed that."

They walked both sides of a corner store that displayed bins of root vegetables alongside bins of flip-flops, turning them down a side street, narrower and lined with mopeds.

"Go on, what was it then?" prompted the other freeformer.

"Oh, disappointment," answered Lis, recalling their prey's puzzling last thought. "That she'd never be a fashion designer. What's a fashion designer?"

Ahead of them, a delivery truck was unloading boxes into an Ethiopian restaurant. The two freeformers walked around, then immediately had to circumnavigate a broken futon frame beside a line of overflowing bins.

"They didn't fill you in on your prey's occupation at the embassy?"

"Embassy?"

The mustached freeformer halted abruptly in front of a cell-phone repair shop safeguarded by diamond-grated windows. He put his head in his hands. Then, just as abruptly, he began walking again.

"There has to be a better system," their companion mumbled to themselves. "You tell them that when you go."

"Go where?" Lis asked.

The freeformer stopped again, this time in front of a hotel that had no other name. Just Hotel. Graffitied garage-door-like shutters concealed its street-level windows.

"Okay, okay, listen. This—" From his pocket, he pulled out a rectangular piece of plastic and held it up in front of Lis' imitated eyes. It was light blue and had the words *Navigo* and *Île-de-France Mobilités* printed on it. "—is your pass to the city. Luckily for you, there's an embassy right here in Paris that's only a metro ride away." The freeformer took a sharp turn back in the direction from which they had just come. Lis hurried to follow. "I'll walk you to the nearest stop. Metro map will get you the rest of the— oh, but you can't read yet."

"I can read."

"Wait, how long did you say you've been human?"

"Just today."

"You're telling me that you learned to read . . . as a dog?"

"The dog's human had a lot of magazines."

"Alright, what does that say?" The freeformer pointed to a red awning shading a glass refrigerator case that showed off the already caught and cut bodies of prey. The sign had a cow on it. Lis hadn't been a cow yet, and now they thought better of it.

"Essaada Butchery."

"Huh . . ." Helmut preened his mustache. "Not often I'm astounded."

As they once again neared the shopping nexus, Lis felt their attention pulled in as many directions as there were details to absorb. Dresses stretched over wide hips and full bellies. Noses pinched, hooked, pierced. Wrists of clinking bangles. Knobby knees poking through ripped jeans. Skulls stuffed in baseball caps, swathed in head scarves, hair styled into a dizzying variety of textures and designs.

The freeformer came to a halt.

They were back almost exactly where they had started. Lis could see the public toilets from where they stood. And where they stood was beside a streetlamp with frosted glass orb and red sign set right into its post that read *METRO*. Said post grew out of a metal railing with only one side open to a set of stairs that descended below the sidewalk.

"You're gonna take Line 4 here towards Bagneux - Lucie Aubrac." The mustached freeformer gestured to another sign, this one of a very complicated looking map, as he proceeded to give equally complicated instructions: "... transfer to Line 9 towards Pont de Sèvres. Get off at La Muette. Got it?" Then he repeated anyway, "*4* to *Strasbourg Saint-Denis* then *9* to *La Muette*."

Lis nodded because they had no need for clarifying questions because they had no intention of going anywhere at present but back to the solitude of their prey's lair to shed their shape. All they had to remember was that the ultimate destination was La Muette, wherever that was. They could figure out the 'how' of getting there later.

"On arrival, you ask someone where the Monaco Embassy is located. Don't look them in the eyes, or the urge to mimic will be irresistible. You will, though, want to imitate the embassy guard's pinky nail, like I showed you."

"I will," Lis assured, hoping to wrap the conversation up.

"Be sure they mimic back before going and gabbing at them in Freespeak. *Verify before voicing!* Just a little aide-mémoire I came up with a while back; feel free to share it with other freeformers you may cross paths with. But only once you ... ?" he trailed off, seemingly wanting Lis to fill in the blank.

"Verify," Lis finished for him. "I will," they repeated to appease.

"Good. Because if you freespeak at a human before verifying, they'll think they're hearing things and more often than not enter a state of complete and utter panic. And a panicking human is a dangerous human."

"I understand," Lis said, edging away toward the metro entrance.

A female human with acne on top of acne walked right between them, shouting at a phone she held at arm's length like an overripe durian. Lis took another step back.

But the other freeformer barreled on: "Once the guard grants you entry, an embassy agent will fill you in on what your prey's occupation was, get you sorted out with money,"—Lis had no idea what 'money' was, but was fine waiting for the embassy to find out—"explain everything you need to know about being human. Well, most everything. Want some free advice?" he asked, then without waiting for Lis to accept, offered it. "One thing they won't tell you at the embassy: humans, they're the biggest parasite on the planet, so, in the spirit of population control, you don't need to wait until you're hungry to catch a prey. Only downside is you *do* grow faster. But start small as you can—" The freeformer gave Lis a disapproving sort of body scan with his mimicked eyeballs. "Unfortunately, you have already outgrown children, but at least this body is petite. Work your way up to the Dutch and the basketball players. Speaking of: sport rules and regulation comprehension will get you a long way towards passing as one of them. Sport and complaining about work. Also, the smarter you are, the more acceptable it is to exhibit excentric behavior, so learn some maths."

"Money, sports, maths, got it." Lis was feeling very overwhelmed again, and not just by the humans swarming all around them. "Thanks," they said by way of 'goodbye' and turned to walk down the metro station stairs.

"Before you go, you got a name?" the freeformer inquired after them.

"Lis."

"Snake?"

Lis nodded.

"My snake name was Sush, though maybe the other snakes called me that because I wouldn't stop hissing. Yup, I've always had a gift for gab."

What's a gab? Lis thought to themselves.

"But since humanhood, I go by my first human child's name, Helmut."

Helmut waved goodbye, and Lis mimicked the human salutation as they descended. As soon as they were out of view of the street above, they stopped.

Lis waited a few minutes there, halfway down the stairs, where they could hear both the commotion of the street above and echoing sounds floating up from below. It was dimmer here, and Lis was tempted to let their features soften—but no, they'd wait until they got back to the solitude of the apartment. They pretended to adjust the laces of their pink tweed boots so that they did not have to look at any humans and their incredible diversity of features as they stomped past in both directions. Down. Up. Up. Down. When Lis presumed enough time must have passed, they followed the up-stomping humans tentatively back into the daylight.

Helmut was not there.

Lis retraced their steps, walking several city blocks to their prey's apartment building. Everything looked different from a taller vantage point. Once or twice, they had to crouch in order to see the street from a dog's point of view and be sure they were, in fact, headed in the correct direction.

***

The moment the apartment door closed behind them, Lis

melted. Literally. Clothes fell into a heap off a body that no longer had the structure of bones to support them.

Lis drooped down to drink out of the dog bowl when they remembered that humans use cups. No one was watching, but they supposed they really ought to get into the habit. They formed an arm of sorts with which they poured the water from the dog bowl into a mug that had been left out on the counter. The dying thought of the dog (whose bowl this had once belonged to) had been, *Ooh, a new friend!* Lis had met them at the dog park, in the bushes where all the canine companions expelled their bodily waste and sniffed each other's expel holes afterwards.

The doorbell rang, and Lis dropped the metal dog bowl with a clatter.

Might it be someone checking on their preyed? Lis didn't want to arouse suspicions by not answering, in particular as whoever this doorbell ringer may be, would have heard the racket just then.

Lis shifted back into form, set their shoulders, and opened the door.

There stood a human male—a fit specimen, dark skin pigmentation contrasted by very straight white teeth—holding a box with a picture of a bone on it. Lis thought they recognized him from when they were the dog. They crouched down slightly to observe him from a lower angle. Yes, the chin stuck out in a very familiar way indeed—

"Oh, I'm sorry!" the human exclaimed, his eyebrows rising. "I didn't know you were . . ." He glanced quickly at Lis' mimicked body then just as quickly averted his eyes.

Curious, Lis too looked down at their human form and became aware of its state of unclothedness. Every animal they had imitated before had worn only skin and hair, though the dog had sometimes been put in a collar and once a bow-patterned bandana at the groomers. Lis had noticed that people liked to use cloth and pigments to embellish themselves, much like the hermit crab uses shells and Coca-Cola bottlecaps.

From behind them, somewhere inside the apartment, Lis heard their prey's phone ring.

One human thing at a time.

Still looking away, the man thrust the box of dog treats in Lis' direction. "For Dogo Chanel."

A gift for them?! "Thank you, I enjoy these." No, these were for the dog who Lis no longer mimicked. They did not have to pretend to like them anymore. "I mean to say that Dogo Chanel liked these."

"Liked?"

"Oh, yes. Dogo Chanel is dead."

"I am so sorry to hear that!" the man exclaimed.

Lis did not know what to say, so they said nothing.

The phone started ringing again.

"Well, you are obviously dealing with . . . a lot, so . . . I'm going to . . ." The man turned around and entered the door directly across the hall and closed it behind him. Lis closed their own apartment door, thinking that they needed much more practice being human if they were ever going to survive undetected.

The ringing had stopped.

Lis slept in the human's bed. It was much more comfortable than the thin, lumpy, worn dog bed that they'd had to curl up on for the past several months.

On the bedside table was the mystifying, glowing thingamajig that their prey had stared at for hours every night like a moth drawn to the light of the moon. She had called it a "laptop." In an attempt to conserve effort, Lis used a soft approximation of a human hand to pry open its screen—otter paw cracking a clam shell—but ended up having to tighten the shape into fingers to enter the password: RokhayaFashionHouse.

As the laptop started up, a little box appeared in the upper righthand corner—[3 Missed Messages]—but then faded away.

Lis maneuvered the arrow to the red, green, yellow, and blue circle they had observed Rokhaya click on hundreds of times, and typed the letters P - A - R - I - S   M - E - T - R - O into the search box.

They fell asleep studying the metro map by the blue light of the screen. When they woke, the light in the room was yellow.

Sounds of a city awake permeated the windowpanes—sounds of potential prey. But Lis had already resolved to go to the embassy before they chanced getting too overwhelmed. They only hoped their second day out in public would prove less challenging than their first.

Lis was sure to cover their skin with clothes. But what clothes? This human had a wide selection of forms and colors from which to choose. Bins overflowing. Heaps of shoes. Garments crammed together so tightly that Lis had to take out a great armful of hangers and dump them on the bed just to be able to sort through the options.

They began by strapping on the breast cage they'd observed Rokhaya wear whenever she dressed up to go out, but Lis couldn't unhook themselves from it fast enough. Instead, they chose a highlighter yellow minidress and paired it with turquoise tights, the logo-patterned shoulder bag Rokhaya never left the apartment without (its purpose yet unknown), and grass green boots with embroidered daisies scattered all over. The boots made a clomping noise as they walked out the apartment door, and nearly tripped over a bouquet of flowers.

Lis picked them up to investigate.

An envelope stuck out of the blooms with the name *Rokhaya* written on it. Lis jammed the flowers between their thighs so that they had free hands to open the card (if it weren't for all this form-covering fabric, they could have simply shaped an extra set). On the front was a picture of a dog with wings and a gold ring floating over its head. It was sitting on a cloud, even though dogs cannot fly. Underneath were the words: *No matter how long we live with them, it's never long enough.*

Lis opened the card. Inside were some pen scribbles which Lis couldn't understand; they hadn't learned cursive yet. But they could decipher that it was signed, in scratchy capitalized letters, *TSITSI.*

They had been so focused on stalking their previous prey that they hadn't bothered to pay much notice to any other human. But now that they thought about it, the neighbor across the hall had stopped by a few times. Perhaps Rokhaya had already started attracting a mate for them.

Lis put the card back in the flowers and the flowers back on the floor. They crossed the hall to the door that they had seen their neighbor—who they now knew was called Tsitsi—retreat into. Lis pressed the little button beside the door and heard a muffled *terriiing* inside the apartment. They waited, but no answer came.

***

This time, with the metro pass Helmut had given them held

tight between their lavender-lacquered fingertips, Lis actually descended the steps all the way down from the city street to beneath it. There, they followed a woman with a large, round tuft of hair atop her head over to a metal barrier of sorts, one in a line, all with clear double swinging doors. Lis was reminded of puffing feathers to attract a mate as a mourning dove. Apparently, humans did that as well. *But not all humans,* thought Lis, looking down at their long burgundy braids.

The puffy-haired woman pushed her way through the barrier. Lis followed— straight into glass. They tried again but could not push past it.

People passed them on either side with a *ting! whunk* of opening doors. Why couldn't Lis penetrate? Could this barrier somehow detect that they were not actually a human? Lis surveyed the barrier-passing humans for a clue and noticed that they were all running their hands along the machines. Hands that all held cards. The same card that—

Lis swiped. The clear doors swung open.

Through the barrier, a tunnel of shiny white tiles dripping with rust led even deeper underground. A nightingalesque song echoed from below. Lis spotted the tuft of hair descending out of sight. They followed into the tunnel but were soon halted with a choice. A split. A ramp to the right. A ramp to the left. They stood between the two choices as commuters streamed by them in both directions. Right. Left. Having studied the map the night before, Lis was utterly and completely confused.

Standing at the split, also, was the origin of the echoey melody. When Lis had been a songbird, to lure a mate they, well . . . Apparently, humans did that as well. But not all humans, thought Lis, considering the mass of tight-lipped commuters. Just like not all songbirds sing to attract a mate. As a great grey shrike, they'd had to catch a field mouse and stick it on a thorn for their desired mate to see. Perhaps these other humans preferred gifts of food? There seemed to be no one way to lure a mate. Hopefully, the embassy could provide more clarity.

Lis approached the singing woman. If they sounded like a songbird, perhaps they had been one?

Lis looked at the fingernail of the hand holding the portable microphone. The nails were painted black and highly chipped. Lis let one of their own lavender nails chip with black polish as they extended their hand to shake, just as Helmut had done with them.

The woman lowered her microphone. "Thank you, but I'm too broke to buy what you're selling, and I've already found Jesus." They did not reciprocate the handshake nor the nail swap.

"Jesus?"

From the look the songbird woman gave her, Lis had said something very wrong. They suddenly felt more of an urgency to get to the embassy. "Which way do I go to Metro Line 4 towards Bagneux - Lucie Aubrac?"

The woman sighed and pointed to the right. As Lis flowed down the right ramp with the pour of people, they heard the echoey voice start back up.

Lis got on the train with a press of other passengers.

The speakers announced: *Attention à vos effets personnels. Attention à la marche en descendant du train. Avant de descendre, assurez-vous de ne rien oublier à bord.* But also, other languages that Lis couldn't understand. *Beware of your belongings. Mind the gap. Before you depart make sure you don't forget anything on board.*

Mochimono ni chūi shite kudasai. Sukima ni kiwotsukete. Shuppatsu mae ni kinai ni wasuremono ga nai koto o kakuninshitekudasai.

The woman directly in front of them was wearing a zebra-striped dress, and Lis had to look away for fear that they might mimic the pattern on their distinctly non-zebra skin. They sat down in an empty seat beside a man whose bulbous nose was nearly touching a portable screen. Across from them, a child with hair in lots of little twists was holding his father's hand with his much smaller one, a finger up his nose. Lis would never be a child now. They wondered if they had indeed been too impatient, like Helmut had said, but then the child's father swatted the child's finger away from his nostril as he spit the word "disgusting!" at him, and Lis decided that they had made the right call after all.

All this observing was tempting Lis to shift form, and there was no public toilet proximate. They averted their eyes to stare at their fellow passengers shoes. The part of them mimicking feet itched.

Lis got out at *"Strasbourg Saint-Denis. Strasbourg Saint-Denis."*

By the time they found their way onto Metro 9, they had to sit with their eyes closed, concentrating on the image of upturned eyes and high cheekbones that they had studied for so long as Rokhaya's canine companion.

Fourteen stops and what felt like forty later, they at last heard: *"La Muette. La Muette."*

There was only one exit on this platform, and Lis took it away from the tracks, up a set of stairs, through more tiled tunnel, past the barricade of metal, and up another set of stairs, exiting into the verdant light of the street above.

The street was different here. Cleaner. Calmer. Its lamps were ornate and painted a velvety dark green. Grand Parisian apartment buildings provided residents with street level bistros, cafés, and creperies. The pedestrian walkways were lined with trees instead of trash. There was a marked lack of mopeds, strollers, and delivery trucks, as well as the humans attached to them. In fact, it was nearly free of humans entirely. Lis caught a brief glimpse of a man in a jumpsuit exit a clean, white van and enter an adjacent clean, white building. Another man down the block in shades of beige was enjoying a leisurely outing with their small canine companion. What a relief it would be to mimic someone less . . . complex.

Lis questioned a couple of humans on where the embassy was located. They were polite and brief in their answers. It wasn't far before Lis was standing in front a brass plaque so shiny that they could see burgundy braids reflected along with the words *Ambassade De Monaco*. The plaque was affixed to the embassy's equally glossy, black iron gate. Closed gate. It guarded a classic Parisian limestone building whose small stature reflected the size of its country, yet stately façade signaled its esteem. Seated just on the other side, a guard. Lis approached. They looked at his hand—fingers thick and stubby with straight-cut nails—and mimicked its pinky. After a moment, his pinky nail grew longer and lavender. Without a word, he opened the gate.

Lis was led by a different guard to a lustrous black door on the side of the building away from the matching front doors that were obviously for show or maybe for the few actual Monaco citizens who lost their passports to pickpockets.

"Identifier?" inquired the freeformer in Freespeak.

"Lis," said Lis.

Inside, they were led down a hall to a room full of chairs that were lined up to all face one way towards a tranquil, bare, black wall. There, they were instructed to sit and wait.

Lis chose a chair apart from the spattering of other occupants. In the seat a few away was an elderly woman in a tutu. Beside her, an adolescent girl with her hair in two messy buns that looked like bear ears. Proximate, a heavily tattooed man in a blue pinstriped suit with matching blue shirt, briefcase, and umbrella.

Lis looked at the black wall.

So peacefully . . . void.

The wall started to play music. A tinkling that repeated in short loops, like a trilling starling call. A call! By the time Lis realized that Rokhaya's phone was ringing in the shoulder bag, it had stopped.

"Lis." A freeformer agent was standing in the doorframe of an adjacent room. They were taking the form of an extremely tall blonde-haired woman in a white blazer and sharply ironed slacks. Lis was envious of the short hair that looked much less complicated to mimic than their long braids, and also a lot lighter.

The room was hardly larger than Rokhaya's closet, but instead of being filled with clothes, it was filled with a table. The walls were painted black, floor and ceiling. Lis felt calm entering it, even as they had to wedge themselves into one of the two chairs at the cramped table.

Lis had barely taken a seat across from the agent when they began asking questions. "What brings you to the embassy today?"

"I was told to come here by another freeformer. Helmut? He said I needed to know some information, since this is my first time being human."

"First time!" The sharp features of the agent's mimicked form softened. "Good. I thought you had an assignment complaint."

"Assignment?"

"You're human now. Humans get assignments. You're gonna have to catch on quick because we have quite a bit to cover and I have a break in twenty."

"Twenty what?"

"Alright, first let's get the paperwork out of the way." She looked down at a clipboard on the table in front of her. The language written on it was not French. "Where do you live?"

Lis handed her the addressed letter.

"Château-Rouge neighborhood . . . Lots of poor immigrants. Displaced. African. Not a lot of questions asked if someone is disappeared," the embassy agent thought out-loud. "And were suspicions to arise, the police there only make things worse, so would almost never be called upon. Good choice."

Lis privately kept to themselves that it had been a pure coincidence that Dogo Chanel had been brought home from the dog park to there.

The agent made a note on the clipboard.

"I'm making this your official assignment for the time being. If you want to change hunting grounds, please return to the embassy and request reassignment. This is important. Too many of us in one location arouses suspicions—humans are the only species to keep death records."

Lis nodded in compliance.

"Prey's occupation?" the agent continued.

"What?"

"Where did she work?"

"Uh . . . she just left every morning and then came back

around evening mealtime."

They made a note.

"What about family?"

"Uh . . ."

"Friends?"

"Uh . . ."

"Did you even stalk this prey?"

"I lived with her for five months."

"Five months! Not very observant, are we?"

"I was a dog. At first, I couldn't understand human vocalizations."

The agent made a disapproving sort of tick on the clipboard.

"But I taught myself to read," Lis offered, remembering how this had impressed Helmut.

"As a dog? Hear something new . . ."

Lis felt a swell of pride.

"Alright," the agent moved on. "Let's look up this . . ." She glanced at the envelope. ". . . Rokhaya Kebe."

She was a runway model. Lis learned that this meant "a fashion professional who showcases clothing, makeup, and accessories from designers." They also learned that one did this for money, and that money was a medium of exchange used to facilitate transactions for goods or services that was worth no more than the value of the collective delusion of its necessity. Also, not to prey on anyone notorious because they would be impossible to imitate credibly under near-constant observation and scrutiny.

"We're still covering tracks from the Tom Cruise fiasco. And don't get me started about Mr. Ye." The freeformer clicked her tongue disapprovingly in a very human way, and Lis wondered how long she had been one; she was very tall. "We will help you prepare to successfully pass as your prey and, when you've moved on to your next, provide a death certificate and cause thereof that would leave no recognizable body."

"That seems like a lot of trouble," Lis said frankly.

"Your safety is our safety. If they ever found out about us, they would turn all resources to destroying us. You are hiding in plain sight among the most dangerous animal on the planet."

"Why are humans the most dangerous animal on the planet?" asked Lis, thinking about a time they saw a lynx rip the jugular out of a caribou.

"They're causing the icebergs to melt."

"Icebergs?"

"Giant chunks of ice."

"Why does it matter if giant chunks of ice melt?"

"The polar bears die. The point is that humans create technologies that pollute, dump islands of trash in the ocean, introduce invasive plants because they look pretty on their front lawn, burn the rainforests, burn holes in the ozone layer, crack the earth open to let out gas."

"Why would they do all that? This is their habitat!" Lis had never come across an animal species that destroyed their own homes.

"Because they burn the gas to make energy."

This species grew more bewildering the more Lis asked.

"Stay with me," the agent said, sensing their trepidation. "Humans are exploiters. They take from nature for food, medicine, entertainment, construction materials. But all they do is take and take and take."

"And so, the icebergs are melting," said Lis, trying to keep up the appearance of keeping up.

"Exactly. They destroy habitats. Half of ALL wild animals are currently at risk, including our great elders, blue whales. As well as those of our kind on their way to elderhood: crocodiles, tigers, gaur, bison, rhinoceroses, ostriches, giraffe, and of course, polar bears. When you outsize your humanhood, revisit here and we'll help place you in a safe host at a protected location: farm sanctuary, elephant sanctuary, orca sanctuary—"

"Why don't we stop them?" Lis interrupted.

"We are. *You* are, now. Those of us in human form are in the best position to protect our formlings and elders—be environmental activists, spread veganism—which is why we try to stay human as long as possible. It is essential some of us are human to protect the rest."

"I understand. What predators should I watch out for as a human?" Lis wondered.

"Only other humans."

"They eat each other?"

"Not usually."

"Then why kill one another?"

"Money, mostly. And jealousy. And greed. And revenge. And pleasure. They kill about half a million of each other a year."

"Amazing they haven't killed all of themselves," Lis marveled.

"They like to mate."

"Well, that's good. Right?"

"For us, yes. Do you have any questions about human mating rituals?"

"Yes," Lis said emphatically. "There seem to be so many ways to attract a mate. Which one is the best?"

"That depends on the individual mate. Do you have one in mind?"

"I do."

***

Lis knocked on the door across the hall. If they were going to prey on this 'Tsitsi' next, they apparently had to do more than just lure them in by posing as a willing mate. *"With humans, you must learn more than their behavior,"* the embassy agent had informed. *"You must learn their interests, their past, their desires for the future, their favorite color."*

The door opened.

Tsitsi was clothed in slacks and a plaid, short sleeve button-up. He seemed taken aback to see Lis, that is, Rokhaya, there.

"Oh. Hello, Rokhaya. How— How are you feeling?"

This was a question Lis had never been asked before. In fact, this was a question they had never asked themselves before, either. How did one express one's emotional state if not by simply *feeling* it through thought?

They must have taken too long to reply because Tsitsi asked another, easier to answer, question. "You received my card?"

"Yes," Lis said. "I liked the picture of the dog." Then out of curiosity, "Why did it have a circle on its head?"

"I believe that was a halo."

"I see. Halo?"

"Uh, it was an angel. A dog angel."

Halo. Angel. All of these words that were unfamiliar. Lis thought it better to pretend to know what this human was talking about so as not to arouse suspicion. The freeformer at the embassy had made it very clear that it was imperative Lis keep their cover—if a human found out they were not one of their kind, they would do more than try to kill them (which had been Lis' only concern before). They would want to capture them, study them, dissect them, expose the rest of their kind. "Yes, of course. Thank you." They would look it up later on the laptop.

There was a pause in the conversation, in which Tsitsi seemed to be waiting for Lis to say something. But what were they supposed to *say*? When they were a newt, all they had to do was a flashy tail dance to attract their mate. Mudskippers have a jumping contest. A cat only has to crouch low and lift their backside into the air. But Lis was supposed to "get to know" a human prey. And the only way to do that? Stalk them.

"I knocked earlier, but you didn't answer."

"I'm sorry. I was— out."

Trying to gather as many factoids about Tsitsi as possible, Lis asked, "Where?"

"Just at the tower."

Lis had no concept of what tower he was referring to. They needed more context. "You like the tower?"

Tsitsi smiled shyly. "I suppose I can't help it."

What did *that* mean?

"Can you show the tower to me?"

"Oh." He looked taken aback again. *What had they said wrong this time?* But then he responded, "Yes, I would be glad to take you there sometime."

"When?" Lis asked so that they would be sure not to be out hunting.

"Well, whenever you are available."

"I am available now."

"Now?"

"Yes." Lis wished they could think this at him instead of resorting to the indistinct and imprecise capabilities of vocalization. In freeformer, 'yes' had many different shades of thought. Some 'yesses' were leaden with obligation. Others cracked open like a door. This 'yes' sparkled like white sand. "Yes, now."

They couldn't tell from Tsitsi's facial expression whether he was surprised in a shining way or biting way.

"I— would like that," he finally verbalized.

"Good. Just one question: are there any public toilets there?"

***

Before Lis even saw the tower, they saw the keychains. They were in the shape of an oddly familiar letter-A-like-symbol that Lis recognized from observing it all around the city: signs, metro posters, even adorning human garments. Men, mostly with dark skin like Tsitsi, like their own, displayed these miniature tower replicas on blankets or carried large metal hoops crammed with them, sometimes multiple hoops around each elbow. They called out prices, *"One euro each!" "Ten for seven!" "Buy two get one!" "Buy five, get three!" "Small one, medium two, large three, all three for four!"* as they followed anyone who let a look linger, even if but for a moment—groups of tourists, mated couples, families with little children asking for souvenirs. Many who seemed interested kept walking by, as if they thought there might be a better deal ahead. Others tried to negotiate. Or pretended to be disinterested until the prices called out got low enough. *"Five for two euro!"*

But none of these vendors approached Lis and Tsitsi as they made their way from the metro station and turned up a set of marble stairs that led to an elevated, expansive, marbled plaza, flanked by great columned buildings and gold statues of humans in varying states of undress. It was crowded with people taking pictures of people posing in front of: the tower.

It had the presence of a black pine.

Lis and Tsitsi passed at least two dozen keychain sellers until, near the end of the plaza, finally one approached. He had three hoops around one elbow and a handful of keychains that he clinked together like a cave of echolocating bats.

"Mhoro, Tsitsi!" the man greeted warmly with a firm handshake and two claps. "Working again?!"

"No, no, just visiting."

The man looked from Tsitsi to Lis and grinned.

"Because you haven't seen this tower enough. But who could get tired of the symbol for *love*?" He winked at Lis.

Tsitsi gave him a penetrating look.

"You work here?" asked Lis. They didn't like the idea of foisting keychains on apathetic pedestrians once they mimicked him—working a prey's job was not something they'd had to worry about as any other species.

"I do." He said it like Lis should already know that. Rokhaya probably would have.

"You haven't seen his paintings? These tourists are buying the next *Mona Lisa*, and they don't even know it!"

"You paint this tower?"

"It's what the tourists want to buy. But for myself, I paint . . . other things."

They moved on towards the tower—a deceptively lengthy walk along a river bridge jammed with beeping cars. Along it, humans called out to each other in clashing languages over the muffled loudspeakers of boats, glut full of tourists, lugging by below. And growing, step-by-step, the metal tree, towering above them. Lis kept their focus aimed up so as to avoid the surplus of form-tempting sights. The tower was so exceptionally big that Lis could be forgiven for thinking it must be close. Yet it took what felt like an age to arrive at the base of the tower, then an age and another just to get through security. When, at last, they were released from the rigid security line, the first thing Lis noticed was a group of humans lying on the ground with arms all stretched up, holding their phones.

"What are they doing?"

"You've never laid down and looked up?"

Lis shook their head 'no,' hoping he would not think it strange that Rokhaya had never done so.

"I know it looks silly and a lot of people think it's just for tourists, but . . . if you don't mind getting a little dusty?"

Lis shrugged. When they'd been a hamster, they'd taken plenty of dust baths.

Tsitsi walked them over to the center of the tower base courtyard. The group was just getting up. He lay down. But he did not hold his phone above him as the tourists had. He only looked up with his eyes.

Lis imitated his behavior and lay down beside him.

Above them was a mesmerizing display of shapes and light. Metal beams crisscrossed to form diamonds and squares and triangles, and peeking through each was a patch of blue, dappled white with cloud. Four great arches marked the edges of their view—the tower was so large that Lis could not see its base from where they lay—and each of these four arches was bordered by an arch of smaller arches and, inside those, smaller arches still. Each looked like a doorway into the sky. It was as if the entire world had disappeared, and Lis could look up, studying this fascinating structure endlessly. It reminded them of flying: the ultimate feeling of freedom (besides melting into goo in a smelly, dark box). And best was that with no human in sight, though they could hear voices echoing from all around them, there was no urge to mimic. Lis felt themselves relax in their human form for the first time outside a toilet.

"I am happy you like the view," came a voice from beside them.

Lis had completely forgotten about Tsitsi in their wonder, and hoped they had not let any of their human features liquesce.

"I can understand why you work here."

Lis suddenly heard the starling-like call, trilling on repeat.

"You can answer that if you want," Tsitsi offered.

The clouds were turning from white to blush pink. The blue sky taking on a purple tinge. "No, that's not necessary." Lis felt like they could study this tower for a very long time—that must be why Tsitsi came here every day to paint it. "Why is this tower a symbol of love?"

"I suppose because many lovers come here. Honeymooners, anniversaries, first dates . . ."

"Have you ever brought a lover here?"

Tsitsi paused before answering. "No. I hadn't— *haven't*— Have you?"

"I have never been in love," Lis responded truthfully, though perhaps Rokhaya had.

"Never?"

Lis needed to know more about love before they could expound on their answer with any accuracy. So, they deflected instead: "Have you?"

Tsitsi sat up beside her.

"Do you mind if we head back? That's a long story, and it's been a long day."

***

Blocking the entranceway to their apartment building, a woman was pressing one of the doorbell buttons repeatedly. Severe white-blonde hair cut straight across the light pink skin of her forehead. The woman looked up as Lis and Tsitsi approached. Her eyes were wolf blue. Lis looked between her eyebrows instead.

"Where have you *been*?" she asked, impassionedly. "I've been calling and calling." She suddenly seemed to notice Tsitsi. "Is *he* the reason why you missed runway? Gabriel was salty as fuck that you ghosted."

Once again, Lis did not know what to say, so, once again, they said nothing.

"Her dog died," Tsitsi offered.

The woman's brow uncreased. "Shit. I'm sorry."

"Yes, Dogo Chanel is dead," Lis said. Apparently, humans were very attached to their canine companions.

"Just— let a bitch know next time. I thought you were dead. And let's grab drinks soon and," she looked pointedly at Tsitsi, "catch up."

"You missed work to be with me?" Tsitsi asked as they walked inside their apartment building, the entranceway now pissed-off-fashion-model free.

In the hallway, outside their respective doors, Tsitsi looked down at Lis' boots with the embroidered daisies scattered all over. "Sorry that today wasn't exactly . . . well, I'd like to take you on a real date, if I may ask . . ."

"A date?" Lis inquired.

"I'm sorry! I clearly read the signals wrong . . ." Tsitsi began to fumble with the keys to unlock his door.

Signals, as in mating signals? If only it was as obvious as a lightning bug signal. All they had to do then was dump some chemicals into their beetle-mimicked butt (but when Lis had tried to see if humans might have such a feature, they succeeded only in peeing themselves.)

"Yes," Lis agreed. "I would like you to take me on a 'real date.'" This 'yes' glimmered like sunlight on lake water.

***

Lis' mimicked fingers pressed the letters D - A - T - E on the laptop keyboard.

1. The day of the month or year as specified by a number

2. A social or romantic appointment or engagement

R - O - M - A - N, they typed, T - I - C

1. Conductive to or characterized by the expression of love

2. Of, characterized by, or suggestive of an idealized view of reality

3. Relating to or denoting the artistic and literary movement of romanticism

L - O - V - E

1. An intense feeling of deep affection
2. A great interest and pleasure in something

Lis was curious about Tsitsi, but they couldn't say they had a deep affection for him.

Lis typed H-O-W T-O F-A-L-L I-N L-O-V-E

The first resource that came up was a 2015 *New York Times* article, titled, "To Fall in Love With Anyone, Do This." Lis clicked the link.

***

Tsitsi was dressed differently for their date. He had on a warm brown suit that looked as crisp as if it were (and probably was) new, and a navy button-up with the top two buttons undone. He wore polished dress shoes and spotless white socks. His teeth looked especially clean, and if Lis could smell, they would have also noted the level of fresh breath that only comes from gargling throat-searing quantities of Listerine.

Lis was wearing the brightest combination of colors they could find in the hopes that this would signal interest.

"You look...vibrant," Tsitsi remarked when Lis opened Rokhaya's apartment door.

"You look clean," Lis replied.

Tsitsi laughed. "Shall we go?"

"We shall. While we commute, can you tell me, given the choice of anyone in the world, whom would you want as a dinner guest?"

"That's an . . . interesting question. Let me think . . ." he said as they exited the apartment building and set out for the nearest, all too familiar, metro stop. "Anyone alive, or in history?"

"I don't know." The article had not specified.

"Well, if historical figures were an option, then it would have to be Monet. His ability to capture light in a simple impressionistic stroke is unparalleled."

"Monet." Filed away. "And would you like to be famous?"

"Like Monet? Who wouldn't?"

The metro ride was noisy and hectic, but Lis still managed to ask, "Before making a telephone call, do you ever rehearse what you are going to say? Why?" as well as "What could constitute a 'perfect' day for you?"

Lis learned that he always rehearsed what he was going to say because he became easily flustered on the phone, and that his perfect day consisted of painting outdoors and something called fried macimbi.

From the metro, they crossed the street and entered an arched tunnel that cut through a palatial building the length of a city block.

"When did you last sing to yourself?"

Tsitsi laughed. "No one has ever paid me so much interest. To be honest, I wasn't sure you had interest in me at all."

They had exited the tunnel. For once, Lis didn't notice the people. The courtyard to the Louvre was vast, and in its center was an angular marvel of glass and light and, they would soon learn, the entrance to the museum.

Lis asked more questions as they stood in the snaking security line inside the glass pyramid. "If you were able to live to the age of ninety and retain either the mind or body of a thirty-year-old for the last sixty years of your life, which would you want?" and "Do you have a secret hunch about how you will die?"

"How do you think of these questions?!" Tsitsi marveled.

Lis did not disclose that they were from "36 Questions That Lead to Love," by psychologist Arthur Aron, as recommended by the "To Fall in Love With Anyone, Do This" article. Nor that they had researched the phenomenon of love thoroughly from the stance of several scientific disciplines: anthropology, sociology, psychology, neuroscience, biology. For biologists, each expression of love had an evolutionary reason: attraction to discriminate in favor of healthy mates, lust to spur reproduction, and attachment for facilitating familial bonding.

Inside, an escalator conveyed them down into the pyramid that grew in size like an iceberg below the ocean surface. An open echoey cavern of dark marble waited at the base. Clumps of humans stuck together. Others were set out on their own. No one seemed to be following any specific path, nor to be headed in the same direction. Except maybe the people stuck looking at the back of the head of the person standing in front of them in one of the staggeringly long lines of aspiring ticket purchasers looking at the backs of each other's heads. A collective, irritated, grumbling murmured in Lis' direction. Thankful that Tsitsi had preplanned and prepurchased, they turned the other way and were at once assaulted by the shrill screams of gleefully misbehaving children. A gush of *awws* broke out at the center of the underground lobby directly under the peak of the pyramid, so high above. Lis shifted their attention over to the commotion and saw a man kneeling on just one knee.

Tsitsi asked something, drawing Lis' attention back to him.

"What?" They had heard the words but had not been able to sift them out of the cacophony of other sounds.

"Anything particular you want to see?" he asked again. "There's Paintings; Prints and Drawings; Egyptian Antiquities; Greek, and then Roman Antiquities; Sculpture, of course; Islamic Art; Near Eastern. Oh yeah, and Decorative Arts. And Etruscan!" he added.

"Whatever you want to show me."

Tsitsi led them up a mountain of marble stairs and into a long room whose other end Lis could not see. It was lit by an arched ceiling of skylights, its walls lined with large gold-framed paintings. Each painting depicted a different scene of humans, many in garments which Lis had not observed before. Others were content to be unclothed, like all other organisms on the planet. Lis found the painted people just as distracting as the live people clustered around each artwork with phones for eyes. Now among the tempting features were nipples and belly buttons and inner thighs. The endless room was broken up by mauve marbled columns that framed massive mirrors. Lis looked at one to their left and was relieved to see Rokhaya's almond eyes staring back at them. Lis made sure to check out their human form every time they passed one such mirror, which helped them maintain it in the mass of luringly mimicable (flesh and paint) faces.

They passed a room on the right that was absolutely packed with museumgoers. Lis hoped they weren't headed there.

"There are far greater works of art than the *Mona Lisa*," Tsitsi said. Then backtracking. "Unless you really want to see it?"

Lis did not know what this *Mona Lisa* was, but they were happy to avoid the many eyeballs viewing it.

"No, I want to see what paintings you want to see."

"This way." Tsitsi started to maneuver them towards the other end of the tunnel-like gallery.

Lis was stopped in their tracks by a small painting of a human made of bark with mushrooms for lips and ivy-covered branches for hair. A second similar painting depicted a face with lips of cherries, teeth of peas, pear chin, peach cheek, and cucumber nose. Alongside it was another plant/human-hybrid, but made entirely from flowers. A fourth had hair of grape leaves and a beard of wheat. Did this artist somehow know about freeformers? Could they themselves have been one?

Tsitsi was back beside them. "Giuseppe Arcimboldo. He painted these in the fifteen-hundreds. That was over three hundred years before Picasso. Three hundred and fifty, I think! To be the first. Imagine."

Lis wondered if they were the first of their kind to try and date a prey instead of eat them.

They walked through a vast maze of rooms, Tsitsi stopping them from time to time to look at a painting, Lis stopping to "use the bathroom" every time they passed one, eventually going down another flight of stairs into a cavern of white marble—white marble walls, white marble statues, white marble framed windows. Lis caught sight of the glass pyramid where they had entered the museum. They were shocked to see the sky behind it purple with a line of orange brushing the horizon. How had so much time passed?

"This . . . is *Psyche Revived by Cupid's Kiss*."

Lis regarded the statue they had halted in front of. A human woman, loosely wrapped in stone cloth, lay on a rock. Above her, a human male—with a pair of wings?—cradled her in his arms. One of his hands was cupping her breast, the other, her head. Both of her arms were stretched up to draw him down closer. Their faces nearly touched. Lis had seen humans touch their faces together in the many movies Rokhaya watched in bed on her laptop. Another of the many mating rituals, no doubt.

Lis became aware of Tsitsi looking at them. Hopefully, they hadn't shown too much interest in what was clearly a statue of a freeformer ensnaring their prey.

"The story goes that there was this prophecy that Psyche," Tsitsi gestured to the woman on the rock, "would grow up to become more beautiful than the goddess of love, Venus. So, Venus ordered her son, Cupid," he indicated toward the winged man, "to make Psyche fall in love with the ugliest being in the world. But Cupid couldn't resist falling in love with Psyche himself. He tried to keep the beautiful princess hidden, but his mother sent her into Hades on a dangerous mission, which caused her to fall into a deadly sleep. Cupid found her and kissed her . . . a kiss that brought her back to life. This is that moment."

So not a freeformer luring a prey.

Lis studied the statue again in the new light of correct context. Psyche was looking up, enraptured by the kiss which had just revived her. Physical love. Lis had never kissed or been kissed before, but it seemed like the thing to do.

Lis positioned their face within touching distance of Tsitsi's face.

He understood the request and pressed, right against theirs, his lips. They were soft and warm and, oh, so bitable.

***

"What did you think?" Tsitsi asked when they exited the museum. Lis was once again surprised by the sky—it was now dark out, and the pyramid was alight.

"When can we go back?" Lis asked in response.

Tsitsi laughed.

"I had the impression that you were more interested in . . . modern trends than classical art."

That might have been true for Rokhaya, but for Lis, "I think I like all kinds of art."

After learning about the horrors committed by humankind at the embassy, Lis had written the entire species off as a lost cause, a planet-wide parasite to be exterminated. But how could a species that could create ART be beyond redemption? Lis now saw the marvelous in them, too.

They looked Tsitsi over, his lips in particular. They thought they might try the kissing thing again when— Tsitsi extended his hand to them.

For a split-second, Lis thought that he was about to reveal himself to be a freeformer in disguise this whole time!

But then he grabbed hold of Lis' hand and . . . held it in his. None of his nails had turned lavender.

***

If you were, say, a fly on the wall of the bedroom that night, you would look away. Not out of modesty (flies famously have none) but out of sheer secondhand embarrassment. For as a fly with no concept of what goes where when mammals do it, you at least would know enough to deduce that it shouldn't be that difficult to figure it out.

Lis and Tsitsi lay beside each other naked and unspeaking in a tangle of sheets.

As a freeformer who had only seen other animals couple, Lis had found it more confusing than it looked. They were well practiced in the art of attracting a mate, but only to lure them in for supper. This was the first time they had let the mating happen to them. And even though they wiggled their body around and made moaning sounds, they had a bad feeling that they had done it wrong. Lis lamented that they should have paid more attention to Rokhaya's inner anatomy before they had consumed her. They had seen the human unclothed enough times, but they didn't know what they were supposed to be like . . . on the inside. But Tsitsi kept pushing and pushing and looking confused, until finally, Lis had allowed the part he was pushing against to press inside. And then he pressed in and out a few times and then it was over, and Lis was stickier than when it had all begun.

It was Tsitsi who broke the silence. "Do we want to talk about what just happened?"

"You don't remember?"

"I kind of wish I could forget, if I am being honest." He looked up at the ceiling. "I had just imagined for so long— it's not your fault. Some people just aren't . . . I just imagined we'd be more . . . compatible."

If they weren't compatible, Lis would have no choice but to eat him. And they discovered in that moment that they had grown too fond of him for that. Perhaps if Tsitsi knew that that was their first time . . . All animals have a first time mating. For some, it is the first of many, like prairie voles or termites. For some, it is the first and last time. Drone bees. Eels. But Lis knew humans mated more than once because they had observed plenty with far more than one grubby, whining, writhing offspring.

"It was my first time. I'm sure it will go more smoothly next time."

Tsitsi sat up.

"Your first— A woman like you— Seriously?"

"Seriously," Lis confirmed, repeating the human phrasing.

"But all the men I saw you bring home . . ."

How could Lis have forgotten. That was how they knew what human mating rituals were supposed to look like, from the outside anyway. They hadn't always had the best view from the lumpy dog bed on the floor. But they had heard the noises they were supposed to make and the things they were supposed to say, like, *"Let me be your fantasy."* and *"Oh, yeah, give me that sugar, Daddy."*

"They were acquaintances," Lis lied.

"So, I was really your first time?"

"Yes," Lis said in all honesty.

Tsitsi leaned over and he hugged them. It was a long hug. A warm hug. Lis found themselves wanting to soften, to melt into it like in a public toilet with nowhere to flush.

Finally, Tsitsi leaned back out of the hug. "I have work early— rent is in three days, you know—but tomorrow night, we will try again, and I will make it special. I promise."

That next night, if you were, say, a fly on the wall, you would be eating a bucket of proverbial popcorn, for Lis had spent the day researching the inner workings of the vulva, and Tsitsi seemed to have made it his personal mission to put his lips on every bit of Lis' mimicked skin.

***

Lis liked dating. It seemed to involve a lot of going places and seeing things at those places. Visiting museums. Exploring historical gardens. Walking the Pont des Arts bridge. Viewing the kaleidoscope of gothic stained-glass inside Sainte-Chapelle. Lis was learning so much about a world that was so much larger than they had ever imagined, even as a migrating bird, and certainly as a worm underground, ingesting dirt and knowing flowers only by their roots! But of the dating activities that Lis ended up enjoying most, most took place right in their territory. Looking for street art. Holding hands at the Le Louxor Palais Du Cinéma. Dancing. They were starting to appreciate the vitality of the Château-Rouge neighborhood with its vibrant colors and music-filled streets. Dating involved a lot of eating, too. So much eating: crepes from street vendors, park picnics, traditional Zimbabwean cuisine. Lis only wished a freeformer could subsist on such foodstuff, but it just passed through their gelatinous innards same as it went in.

There was also a lot of mating, which Lis found unexpectedly pleasurable, though they would never admit that to another freeformer. Mating with an inferior species, well, it was so unheard of that there had as of yet not been a need to label the act taboo.

Then there was the talking. Talking while they went to the places and looked at the things. Talking after mating (and during, too).

"If you were to die this evening with no opportunity to communicate with anyone, what would you most regret not having told someone? What haven't you told them yet?" This was question number 33.

"You first," Tsitsi deflected. Whenever Tsitsi asked these questions back at them, Lis would answer as if they were Rokhaya as best they could, but most answers they had to flat out make up.

Lis could not tell Tsitsi what they had not told him yet. "I asked you."

"Here it goes, then. I would regret not telling you— that I love you."

"You do?" Lis enjoyed Tsitsi's companionship and were always curious to learn more about him, but no more than they had with Rokhaya. Lis was not sure yet if they were in love or just in love with the idea of it.

"You don't have to say it back."

So, Lis didn't.

Later, by the light of the laptop, Lis looked up B - O - O - K - S A - B - O - U - T L - O - V - E

****

The following weeks, Lis read *Sense and Sensibility* by Jane Austen, *Love's Labour's Lost* by William Shakespeare, *Lady Chatterley's Lover* by D.H. Lawrence, *Lolita* by Vladimir Nabokov, *The Anatomy of Love* by Helen Fisher. But the more they learned about love, the more they questioned whether they felt it.

They also finished asking the 36 Questions, with: "Share a personal problem and ask my advice on how I might handle it."

"I want to know if I should keep trying to be a painter, or if I should go get a more conventional job that earns more money, so that maybe . . . I can afford to have a family one day." The questions seemed to have worked for him. "How do you think I should handle this?"

But all Lis could think about was how delicious his lips looked as he talked. They couldn't help but imagine their own lips swelling with the fullness of his after a fresh meal.

Lis was getting hungrier.

And if Lis was hungry, that meant that other freeformers out there were also hungry. And hunting.

They found themselves checking up on Tsitsi at work between their own modeling gigs (which were few and far between. Apparently, if you didn't actively seek work as a runway model, you wouldn't have any). Anyone that approached to look at his paintings might be a predator. And Tsitsi was such an unsuspecting prey.

"You don't have to keep coming to work with me. I know it's boring."

"Oh, I find it quite . . . stimulating," Lis said as they subtly mimicked the pinky nail of the backpacker they spotted approaching. A signal that they had claimed Tsitsi as their prey, should they be a freeformer.

The backpacker did not look at Lis' pinky nail. He did admire Tsitsi's work. Even had a conversation with him about where he was from and their shared ambition to attend an art academy, but he didn't buy anything.

***

Tsitsi asked one day if he could paint Lis' portrait (or a portrait of Lis wearing Rokhaya's appearance).

Lis sat and watched him mixing colors and taking them to the canvas one after another—browns, ochre, burgundy, red—none of which would have been used if Lis were in their true form.

"What's your favorite color?" Lis asked, thinking of the embassy agent as they did so.

"That's a tough question for an artist," said Tsitsi, pausing with his brush on the canvas. "But I suppose I have a certain fondness for vermillion. What's yours?" he asked, turning his attention back to the stroke of his brush.

Was he asking Lis or Rokhaya?

The doorbell again. Lis thought they'd very much like to break it.

There, a human female with flabs of leathery tan skin and sleek black hair. Another fashion model?

"It's Helmut," the woman offered in Freespeak before Lis could ask.

Helmut? The freeformer from the public toilet! The freeform er . . . here . . . with Tsitsi just inside.

"Oh, hello. What . . . are you doing here?"

"I've been away. Libya. It was great. No one gives a shit how many people disappear there. Assume they've been detained or died in the desert. And the best part was there are tons of areas to go au naturel, even outside in daylight—desert for days! Speaking of, I need to get out of this shape pronto." Helmut pushed past Lis and into the apartment. "Oh, hello," Helmut said out loud. "You didn't tell me you had company."

Helmut was looking at Tsitsi, who was still standing at his portable easel across the room by the window.

"Hello?" said Tsitsi.

"This is my neighbor," Lis explained so Helmut wouldn't think Tsitsi a fellow freeformer.

"Tsitsi," said Tsitsi, putting down his brush and wiping his hands on a rag.

Helmut walked over and shook Tsitsi's hand. "Fatimah."

"Yes, Fatimah," said Lis.

"Former neighbor," said Helmut, obviously more practiced in the art of identity crafting.

"So, what are you doing back, then?" Lis asked, trying their best to sound unconcerned.

"I missed the challenge of the city." Helmut didn't take Fatimah's eyes off Tsitsi. "I need somewhere to crash until I find a new . . . place."

Lis knew that 'place' was code for 'prey'.

"He's my next prey," Lis lied in a voice only Helmut could hear. "I've been stalking him for weeks, and I'm hungry. So, I'm sorry, but you'll have to find someone else."

"Ach, he's too small for me! But he sure looks like a tasty morsel." Fatimah licked her lips. Tsitsi looked somewhat alarmed.

"So," Helmut pivoted, "how are you finding being human?"

"It's a lot," Lis confessed. "A lot of humans. A *lot* of variety. It's been hard to resist mimicking. How do you manage?"

Tsitsi, not realizing that Lis and Helmut were speaking, cleared his throat. "So, I guess I'll leave you two to catch up . . ."

Lis was glad for Tsitsi to depart. It was safer for him that way. "Alright."

"See you later," Tsitsi said. And then, in front of Helmut, he kissed Lis on the lips.

The moment he was out the door, Helmut turned on Lis, arm fat flapping.

"Why did that human kiss you?"

"I've been luring him. That's all."

"With your *body*?" Helmut's thoughts dripped putrid with disgust.

"He's not disgusting," Lis found themselves thinking defensively.

"Oh," Helmut sat down, sinking so deeply into the couch that he might as well have been sitting on the floor. He shook Fatimah's head, and her chins wobbled. "You've formed an attachment with the human, haven't you?" And without waiting for the answer: "Listen, humans, they may hold a certain . . . exotic appeal . . . but you can't keep one as a pet. They're too dangerous."

"Tsitsi isn't dangerous. He . . . loves me."

Helmut laughed and laughed and laughed, his lard-filled breasts bouncing against the blubber of his substantial stomach.

"It loves who it thinks you are. It can't really love you if it doesn't know your true nature."

***

"Do you agree that you can only love someone if you know their true nature?" Lis asked Tsitsi.

It was the next day, and Lis had snuck across the hall while Helmut was sleeping off their recent high-fat meal.

Tsitsi was cleaning his paint brushes in a jar of murky liquid (that would have smelled of paint thinner could Lis have smelled it) but at the question, he paused and considered. "Yes, I think true love is honest love."

"Honest . . ."

"Why?" He set his brush down.

"I have not been . . . honest . . . with you. About who I am."

Tsitsi walked over to where Lis sat on his pull-out sleeper sofa. "Whatever it is, you can tell me." He sat down beside them.

"It's hard to explain . . . Can I show you?"

"Okay . . . ?"

Lis stood up and positioned themselves directly in front of Tsitsi. If they were honest about themselves, then maybe they would *finally* feel that elusive emotion called love.

Lis closed their eyes to shut out any visual distractions. Let their body relax. They imagined a blue sky without a cloud and let themselves expand into it. They felt features melt, boundaries soften. As their eyelids dissolved, Tsitsi came back into view. His own eyes were wide and unblinking, his jaw was slack. He drew a deep breath in, and then he started breathing in and out very rapidly and very heavily. His jaw started moving. "Wha . . . wha . . . wha . . . ?"

"I'm a freeformer," Lis said in Freespeak.

Tsitsi clasped his head with both hands. Suddenly, he was standing. "Did you just speak into my head?" He scrambled backwards and knocked over a lamp. He let it fall as he backed into a wall.

"We speak with our thoughts because we do not always have mouths," Lis thought to him.

"Can you stop? Please?!" Tsitsi pleaded, cowering in the corner.

If he loved them then, he would accept them with or without a mouth—perhaps Helmut had been right, thought Lis heavily.

"Helmut?" asked Tsitsi.

Lis must have been thinking out loud.

Lis turned their attention to the painting of Rokhaya on the easel. They concentrated on the long braids, the upturned brown eyes, and felt themselves tighten and take form once again.

"Helmut is a freeformer acquaintance of mine," said Lis with their mouth, since they now had one again. "You know them as Fatimah."

Tsitsi's head kept cocking to the side. Then he started nodding and nodding. Then he stopped nodding. Held his head perfectly still. Eyebrows furrowed.

"Have you always been . . . Rokhaya?"

"I have been many creatures. But most recently, I was Dogo Chanel and then I was Rokhaya."

"Were you this, when we . . ."

"Mated? Yes."

"Are you an alien?"

"Alien?"

"From another planet?"

"Like another Earth?" Lis' world expanded even more.

"No. Ok, not an alien—" Tsitsi stood up and started pacing back and forth in front of the sofa. "What happened to Rokhaya and Dogo Chanel, when you took their form? Did . . . did you kill them?"

"Well . . . yes. But only because I was hungry."

Tsitsi stopped in his tracks. "You *ate* them?"

"Yes. Don't you eat other creatures when you are hungry?"

"That's different."

"How?"

Tsitsi started pacing again.

"Are you going to eat me?"

"I was going to, but I have decided to love you instead."

Tsitsi started to nod his head again. "This is . . . a lot . . . to process. Do you mind if I go . . . for some fresh air?"

"I do not mind." Lis moved toward the door.

"Alone?"

***

Tsitsi was still gone for some fresh air when the sky darkened. He was still gone when the streetlamps came on and when lights in the apartment building across the street went out.

What if he had gone to the human policing agency? Lis kept this thought to themselves for fear of what Helmut might do if he knew what Tsitsi knew.

Helmut was still taking up residency in Rokhaya's apartment. Lis dreaded seeing him but also did not want to give him reason to suspect that anything might be amiss. So, they left Tsitsi's apartment and crossed the hall. They would tell Helmut that Tsitsi was asleep and that he had to go to work early the next day. They would spend the day helping Helmut find a new prey to stalk, though Lis secretly wondered if they would find any human blubberous enough.

But when Lis finally mustered up the courage to open the door, Helmut was not there.

What if he had overheard Lis talking to Tsitsi in Freespeak? What if he had gone after him? What if he had found him?

When it was officially the next day, but not yet morning, Lis knocked on Tsitsi's door and, when he didn't answer, used the key on the top of the door frame to let themselves in. But Tsitsi was not there, either. Not under the covers. Not behind the sofa bed. Not curled up in any of the kitchen cabinets like a raccoon in their den. On their way out, Lis opened the coat closet. But instead of Tsitsi, or even coats for that matter, they found only a closetful of canvases. All portraits. All of Rokhaya. Paintings he must have completed long before Lis had taken her form. With no sign of the artist in question, Lis closeted the paintings once again.

If you were, say, a fly who had hurled themselves against the window for so long that all you had energy to do was to sit on its sill and stare, you would see Lis restlessly popping between apartments. Still no Helmut, still no Tsitsi, still no Helmut, still no Tsitsi . . .

Lis paced back and forth across the hall—anxious whenever they tried to settle—for what felt like hours. But eventually, they wore themselves out and curled up on Rohkaya's light pink velvet couch, staring unblinkingly at the door.

***

Lis woke to the doorbell.

Tsitsi was on the other side. His face was puffy. His eyes bloodshot.

"Can you be a bird?" he asked.

"I can't anymore—too much mass. But I have been."

"What's it like? To fly?"

Tsitsi and Lis talked for hours. He was hungry for answers, almost hungry as Lis was for a new form.

"How do you decide who to imitate?"

"By size mostly. One day I will be a whale."

"Why do you have to . . . consume . . . who you imitate?"

"Because I am hungry." That much, Lis thought, should be obvious.

"But— I've seen you eat! That time we went to African Kitchen. And the picnic by the Seine."

"When I eat this dead food, my body cannot absorb the nutrients. Like an animal eating pebbles."

"So . . . you have to eat *live* animals?" Lis noticed an involuntary shudder vibrate Tsitsi's muscles. "But . . . if you can eat animals, then— why eat . . . us?"

"Humans are animals." Lis had thought Tsitsi more intelligent than this.

"Technically, yes, of course," Tsitsi conceded. "But we are also more— we have morals and . . . a sense of mortality! Humans are the smartest species."

"Humans also have the most power of any species. It is our duty to imitate humans as long as possible so that we can protect the planet from them." Lis said, repeating almost word for word what the embassy agent had explained to them.

"But why? Why can't you eat another species but just keep this human body?"

"If I eat another species, I will have to take the appearance of that species."

"I can't date an animal!" Tsitsi started shaking his head again.

As calmly and reassuringly as Lis could, they said, "Then you will have to date me in another human body."

"But *why*?"

"If I don't mimic the human I consume, then their disappearance could be noticed. Our kind could be discovered. And if we didn't consume humans at all, then none of us would be one to protect the others."

"Don't you feel guilty, though?"

"Guilty?"

"Wouldn't you feel better if you killed someone who deserved it? Who was a bad person?"

"Bad, like destroying our planet?"

"Sure."

"Then all humans are 'bad persons.'"

Tsitsi stood suddenly and started gesturing. "I meant murderers. Morally corrupt. Pedophiles! Rokhaya didn't deserve . . ." Tsitsi sat back down.

"This is my first time being a person, so I didn't really choose. Dogo Chanel just happened to be owned by Rokhaya."

"Well, I'd rather you eat me than someone else," Tsitsi asserted, crossing his arms.

Tsitsi went on and on about morality and murder and something called 'vigilante justice.' But Lis was so preoccupied with their hunger, they had a hard time concentrating on anything else. They found themselves agreeing with him, without knowing exactly what they had agreed to.

And then, Tsitsi was assuring them, "I'm sure we can find someone with a corrupt soul."

The door opened without warning, and the flabby form of Fatima squeezed through the frame.

"Where were you?" Lis asked in Freespeak. The question was nervous, like a mouse in an open field.

But Helmut responded out loud. "I was just taking in the city. But this body is slower moving than when I was . . . young." Lis knew he meant when he was in a smaller form, and now Tsitsi knew, too, but Helmut didn't know that, and Lis would make sure he never would.

Helmut heaved Fatimah's body over to the couch and sat down next to Tsitsi. "You two are up early."

"Tsitsi has to work—rent . . ."

Catching on, Tsitsi stood. "Yup, I had better get ready for work."

The moment Tsitsi closed the door behind him, Lis asked: "Did you go to the embassy?"

"They wouldn't like this at the embassy," Helmut said.

"So you didn't—"

"Like I told the human: just out for a stroll/stretching the body."

"You don't have to tell them," Lis suggested.

"I don't *have* to," Helmut agreed.

***

Now that Tsitsi knew who Lis was, he showed even more of an interest in them. He wanted to know their real name, what animals they were and what each experience had been like, how Lis knew how to mimic, and how freespeak worked. He seemed even more excited to show Lis things they had never seen before— *"This is a telescope!"*—and take them places they had never been before—*"Wait until you see the hall of mirrors in Versailles!"*—and give them experiences they had never tried before—*"This means you have never listened to a Bob Marley album!"*

But Lis found they had less and less energy with which to enjoy the world. A dullness started to settle over them. They needed to relieve their shape more frequently and lingered in the dark longer each time. Lis was hungry. And not just for food, but for vitality.

Tsitsi had found them plenty of prey—"morally corrupt souls," as he put it—but many were either on their way to, or already in, prison. Among other prospects, high-profile politicians and people listed on the national sex offender registry.

Lis thought he better find them an appropriate prey soon, because there was only so long that they could resist the cravings, and Tsitsi was looking more and more appetizing by the hour . . .

***

"I found her!" Tsitsi exclaimed.

She had a blog on why immigrants should be forcibly removed from French soil, but only a few followed it. No one but

Islamophobes and internet trolls would notice or care if she up and stopped posting. There was enough egomaniacal biographic information on the blog that Lis would not have to waste more time stalking her. Finally, a prey that had potential.

Plan was pretend to be a like-minded podcaster, invite her to an interview that no person who thinks so highly of their opinion that they put every little thought that passes through their head on the internet would be able to resist, and once they'd been lured, eat.

"Do you find her appearance sexually appealing?" asked Lis, studying the picture of the round-faced, pink-skinned female with hair in a French twist that showed off pearls studding each ear lobe, and who looked very different from Rokhaya.

Tsitsi pulled at his collar and cleared his throat. "I mean, well, she's not you, but—"

The apartment door opened again without so much as a knock, and a large man wedged his way in sideways. His skin may have been the color of Tsitsi's, but he was a good five times his size. Helmut had eaten again. If Lis had a stomach, it would have rumbled.

Lis stood. "I'm sorry, but I can't have you stay here anymore," they thought at Helmut. Firm, but not forceful. "Didn't this new prey of yours have a home?"

"You're kicking me out?" Helmut asked incredulously.

"I just need my space."

"You mean *we*."

"Yes," Lis asserted. "*We* need our space."

"There will be more space if you just get it over with already and eat him." Helmut took a massive floor-shaking step in Tsitsi's direction. Tsitsi took two steps back.

"You are not welcome here anymore. Get out."

Lis wasn't sure if they'd be able to protect Tsitsi if Helmut decided to attack. But he only smirked and waddled out without a word.

"Helmut— Fatimah, will be after us now, probably on orders from the embassy . . . We need to act fast."

"Tomorrow," promised Tsitsi. "Right now—" he moved closer. "I'd like to enjoy this body one more time."

As they mated, Lis felt the vigor of his thrust, the flex of his back muscles, pulse of his jugular. Lis wrapped their mimicked arms around him, like Psyche drawing Cupid in for another kiss.

And like Cupid waking Psyche from a sleep akin to death, Tsitsi looked down at them.

"You know how you asked if true love needs to be honest? Because you've been honest with me, I can now say that I truly love you, Lis."

He had called them by their freeformer name.

For the first time, Lis looked Tsitsi in the eyes.

His irises were made up of earthy ridges and ravines so deep that you'd have to dive in to see the bottom—and Lis had an irresistable urge to leap . . .

Lis felt their shape soften. And let it. Let their freed form wrap around Tsitsi's solid one. He was squirming and flexing, and his mouth was sucking, sucking. Lis swathed the entire surface of his body with the gelatinous blanket of their own. Every angle, every pore. Within a minute, he had stopped resisting.

They digested the skin first, slurping out hair and gummy keratin-coated roots and pouring into the emptied follicles.

They tasted the tang of nerves and absorbed the swell of blood that erupted through ruptured veins. They licked over tissue and ligaments and joints. Lis wanted to savor them each. Each unique delicacy. Each pop of tendon and deliquescence of muscle. Bones dissolved. The skull cracked open. A great gulp of brain swelled into Lis' body, and they tasted that juiciest of last thoughts.

You hear the door across the hall open and close. You grab your stack of paintings resting by the apartment door and open your own. Rokhaya is just finishing locking her apartment. She turns and you almost give up before you even try. She's so out of your league.

"Hello," you manage.

"Tsitsi," she acknowledges.

"Just going to work," you say, lifting up your stack of paintings. She does not inquire about them, like you had hoped. Like you had fantasized.

"Same," she says. "Late as usual!" She walks down the hall, heels clomping with the confidence of a model. You feel that you are not invited to walk with her. You lock your door, feeling a fool.

***

You shake your head as you press Rokhaya's doorbell. You hold the box of dog treats in your hand like a shield.

The door opens, and there is a body even more perfect than you've imagined. And you've imagined.

"Oh, I'm sorry!" you hear yourself say. "I didn't know you were . . ." Look away, you should look away!

Her body reminds you that she's not out of your league, she's out of your stratosphere. Why would she answer the door like this? Was she expecting someone else? One of the men you see her with sometimes? The ones with clean shoes.

You hold out the box of treats. "For Dogo Chanel."

"Thank you, I enjoy these," she says. She does not sound embarrassed that she is naked. Modesty is obviously not part of the model job description. "I mean to say that Dogo Chanel liked these."

"Liked?" you ask. Oh no, oh no, oh no . . . Your gesture was about to backfire, you can feel it com—

"Oh, yes. Dogo Chanel is dead."

***

You open your door and there is Rokhaya. She is wearing clothes this time. An odd assortment. Must be coming from an avant-garde photo shoot.

***

You lie under the Eiffel Tower and look over at Rokhaya. She is looking up in awe.

***

Life imitates art as you are revived by Rokhaya's kiss. It is exactly what you fantasized would happen when you brought her to see the marble statue. But even better; she kissed you first.

***

Rokhaya gave up her virginity for you? All the aloofness, the sex appeal, it was only a façade. Disappointment is replaced with honor.

***

Everything Rokhaya does, it is like a child trying something for the first time. Food. Dancing. Art appreciation. If you didn't know any better, you would think she'd led a sheltered life. Experiencing the world with her is like seeing it new again.

***

Rokhaya melts before your eyes. Her clothes lose shape. You can see through her! You want to scream, but no noise comes out.

***

You walk the streets, letting your feet take you anywhere but back home.

Rokhaya is a shapeshifter. Rokhaya is dead. A shapeshifter is Rokhaya. A shapeshifter?! Her skin dissolved before your eyes. That thing inside, that sluglike gelatinous . . . blob . . . you had sex with that— Does the government know about this? Should you tell someone? What would happen to Rokhaya—the thing impersonating Rokhaya—if you did?

You walk the streets for hours, but eventually you find that your feet have walked you back to her apartment door.

This soul you fell in love with, it is clear that it was not Rokhaya. It was this shapeshifter who moved through the world with wonder and curiosity and genuine interest in you.

But she ate Rokhaya, you think.

Rokhaya, who clearly thought she was better than you.

But Dogo Chanel!

Still, you find your hand lifting to the doorbell and pressing.

***

You think that Lis must be the most amazing woman—being— in the world. She is quirky and silly and curious and passionate. Not the woman—whatever—you thought you'd end up with. But what in life ever goes as expected?

***

You feel as if your skin is being slathered in a thick mucus. You open your mouth to scream, only for it to be filled with Lis' liquid body. You taste watermelon, strangely.

If you could have, you would have shouted: "Please stop! Let me help you find someone else! I'm sorry you are so hungry! I love you!"

Then you remember that Lis' kind speaks with thought. So, you think as hard as you can, "I love you! Please stop!" But either Lis cannot hear you or does not care for pleading.

Your lungs burn. Your heart pounds against your crushed chest, which heaves as if you were gagging. A boiling panic spreads through your body. Your temples throb. Your brain swells against your skull, which might be cracking under the pressure of the pressing, squeezing mucus.

This is how you die.

Not as a famous painter, but as food.

Your lungs have stopped contracting. In a detached, observational sort of way, you feel the body that was once yours stop fighting. A darkness blankets you. A calm settles. A feeling that at least, in your death, you are feeding the one you love. What better reason to sacrifice your life?

Lis lapped up the last of the creamy marrow along with the always bizarre feeling of dying—no matter the species or the circumstance, every single creature is surprised when their time finally comes. Satiated once again, they flexed themselves into the shape of Tsitsi. Defined muscles, lustrous skin, mouth of straight white teeth. They felt new, and not just because they had this new form.

"Oh," Lis said, "so that's what love feels like."

HAPPINESS IS FOR
PRETTY PEOPLE

Eric Sterbenk

Olivia scrolled on her phone. TikTok, Instagram, Snapchat, TikTok again. Over and over and over. Videos of people with beautiful hair, beautiful boyfriends, beautiful lives. She had tried doing the makeup and the hair like they did, but it was hard and expensive and she gave up. It was dumb, anyway; there's no way she could ever look like they do, walk like they do. She was too tall, too gawky, too awkward. She switched to her camera on her phone and looked at herself. She hated her hair—it was too brown, too curly, too much. She hated how tall she was—people always looked at her funny, asked her if she played basketball. She switched back to Instagram and kept scrolling.

"OLIVIA!"

Startled, Olivia looked up and saw a customer at the counter. Her co-worker, Jason, stood in the back of the shop, mopping, and looking at her, annoyed. She was supposed to be covering the front while he mopped. The floor didn't need mopping anyway. It was fine. Why did he have to leave her at the front counter alone?

"Sorry," she said, unfolding herself from her phone and stepping to the counter. "What do you want?"

The woman didn't reply immediately, and Olivia stared at her. The woman—a fat older woman, oh my god, she should get a haircut from this century and that dress, how horrible, is that a muumuu in the worst shade of green—stared at the menu, having not made up her mind even after waiting all this time. "What do you recommend?" she asked.

Olivia stared at her. "I don't drink coffee."

"All right, a cappuccino please." The lady smiled, trying to make nice. Olivia didn't respond. Why do people always want to make nice with the baristas at coffee shops? She wasn't here to be friends.

"We don't have those."

The lady points to the menu on the wall above Olivia. "But . . . it says it right there, on the menu."

"We're out."

"You're out? How can you be OUT of Cappuccino?"

"The machine is broken." Out of the corner of her eye, she could see Jason roll his eyes.

"Fine, just a coffee, then, thank you."

Olivia handed her an empty cup and pointed to the wall behind the customer, where a line of coffee thermoses stood. Jason had just refilled them, she knew. "Coffee is self-serve. That'll be $5.50"

Muumuu woman handed her the money, and Olivia rang her up. The woman turned, the floral print dress flapping in her wake, and looked at the three flavors of coffee, trying to make another decision. OMG, just pick one! Like Olivia would make a cappuccino for a woman like that, who was too dense to realize that the coffee was only three dollars. Olivia slipped the difference into her pocket, making sure that Jason didn't see her do it.

Olivia sat back on her stool, watching the woman try to pick a flavor. The music player in the shop had been broken for a while. The only sound in the room came from the swish of Jason's mop, back and forth, and muumuu lady tapping her fingernail on her front teeth, trying to pick the best flavor. The air in the room was so suffocatingly still, it made Olivia want to scream.

But she didn't. She curled up around her phone and scrolled and scrolled and scrolled. One day, she would get out of this shop, this town. Soon.

The bell over the door chimed. Olivia looked up, involuntarily, and saw the muumuu lady standing there, about to leave. She looked at Olivia for a moment, and then shook her head, a sad but oddly hungry look on her face. "You're not happy, are you?" the lady said. Olivia opened her mouth to tell the lady to fuck all the way off but she was out the door, her green floral muumuu trailing behind her as the door slammed.

Olivia, unsettled, looked at Jason, but he was wordlessly mopping the floor, still. What the fuck did that mean, was she happy? No, she wasn't happy, but that wasn't any business of muumuu lady. Was muumuu lady happy? How could she be, looking like that? Almost unconsciously, Olivia reached for the security of the cash in her pocket. Fifty, maybe sixty dollars she had skimmed this morning. At this rate, she had one week, maybe two, and she would finally have enough. She wasn't stupid. For an apartment in the city, she needed first and last month's rent, enough money for bus fare, and enough for food for the first month. She'd figure it out from there. She had scoured the apartment listings, trying to figure out what was good, what was normal, what she could afford. She had found one place, in Williamsburg—a studio apartment. She opened a browser, clicked on the bookmark to the listing. Studio apartment, third floor walkup, above a bodega. The sidewalk outside was full of people, there was a pizza joint and a yoga studio on the block, and a few real estate offices. Nothing fancy, but safe, she thought, and not here. It wasn't available anymore, but she knew there would be more like it—a place of her own, a place without her mom and her lame hobbies, or her sister and her brainless boyfriends.

She found her stool in the corner again, curled around her phone, and scrolled and scrolled and scrolled.

***

Olivia slipped through the front door, quietly shutting it behind her. Maybe, just maybe, she could make it to her room without having to deal with her mom or her sister. The house was weirdly quiet, though. She stepped over an empty delivery box, just the latest one that littered the living room and the driveway. Her mom's latest attempt at making it rich—making her own jewelry and selling it. She'd save more money if she learned to cook and clean, but what did Olivia know, she was only eighteen. The place smelled of old french fries and cat litter. Where was Smokey, anyway? He normally was all over her the minute she walked in.

"Smokey?" She looked in her mom's room. He could be anywhere in there—the room looked like a tornado had swept through it, with clothes and boxes strewn everywhere. Olivia moved a few boxes around, looking for him, but found no sign of the black and white cat. Weird.

They lived in a small ranch-style house, barely bigger than a trailer. Her mom got the house in her parent's divorce, and Olivia had often wondered if it would have been better if she hadn't—her mom might have had to get a real job. Olivia had insisted on the last room down the hall, even though it was the smallest, because it was the furthest away from the chaos and noise and stupidity of her family. Passing by her sister's room, she reached her door . . . which was slightly open. She never left her door open. She pushed the door open the rest of the way, looking around . . . no. They couldn't have. Her room was neat, everything in its place, just like she left it, just like she usually had it—except on her bed was the cigar box she had been saving her escape money in.

Empty.

"No, no, no, no, this can't be happening," she said out loud to no one. She upended the cigar box in the futile hope that something would fall out, even though the box was clearly empty. Olivia sat on the bed, cradling the box in her lap, cradling the anger building in her chest, looking around the room, desperately hoping maybe the money was just sitting out somewhere. Was it her mom? Or her sister? Furious, she reached for her phone and started to text her mom, when she heard the scrape and clatter of the screen door opening.

"Mom?" Olivia shot up and bolted down the hall. Her mom and sister were coming into the kitchen. Her mom was carrying a cat carrier, which was suspiciously quiet—Smokey hated the cat carrier. Her sister followed closely, carrying three bags of takeout food and sipping on an extra-large soda.

"Here you go, Smokey, you're home now," her mom cooed at the cat carrier. Her sister sat down and started pulling food out of the bags, stuffing a handful of fries into her face as she did so.

"Mom, what happened to my . . ."

Her mom interrupted her. "Oh, honey, you won't believe it. Right after you went to work this morning, that pit bull next door got loose and attacked Smokey! But she's ok now, thank goodness. The vet fixed her right up."

Olivia looked into the front of the cat carrier. A bundle of bandages in the approximate shape of a cat lay against the side of the carrier. Except for the small black ear with white tufts in it sticking out, Olivia couldn't have been sure that it was even their cat.

"Ok, but, did you go into my . . ."

"Sweetheart, I'm so sorry. It was a life or death situation. Don't you see?" Looking ashamed, her mom reached out to put a hand on Olivia's arm. Olivia snatched her hand away. Her sister took a big sip of her coke, watching the exchange, delighted.

"You took my money?" Olivia's voice shook.

"Wasn't yours," her sister said, monotone, grabbing another handful of fries. "You stole it."

"That was MY MONEY!"

"It's only a loan, honey. I'll pay you back. I promise." Her mom, to her credit, looked a little ashamed. "This next set of necklaces that I designed are going to be big sellers. We had to save Smokey. Don't you understand?"

Olivia understood. She understood that she would never get out of this town. She understood that her family was useless and would keep her in this house, this town, this life, forever. She spun on her heel and stomped down the hallway.

"Are you gonna eat your fries?" her sister called after her. Olivia screamed, incoherent and raw and full of rage, and slammed the door behind her.

***

The coffee shop was busy. Olivia hadn't even had time to check her socials. She'd been slammed the whole morning—all the insipid bros on their way to work in the finance district, their hair slicked back, Patagonia vests on, ordering a "flat white" like it made them cool. Fucking capitalists, ruining the world one over-hyped buzzword at a time, all so the patriarchy could have another fat white man buy another BMW. She was so busy she had forgotten to overcharge them and pocket the money—and besides, she was working with Peggy this shift, and Peggy had seen her slipping some money into her bag the other day. Olivia had explained it away, but the way Peggy watched her at the cash register—maybe today wasn't the day to be risky.

Just thinking about the money made the simmering resentment and fury at her mother and the world come to the surface, and she had to bite back what she really wanted to say to the customers in front of Peggy. The counter cleared, and she had just settled into her spot on the stool, about to sink into the dopamine-fueled numbness of scrolling on her phone when the bell over the front door chimed.

Olivia sighed and looked up to see an older man, much older, come through the door. A group of older folks came in every morning and sat in the cafe and talked and laughed and took up space after ordering the cheapest items on the menu. They didn't have much time for Olivia, and the feeling was mutual. But this guy wasn't part of that crew. He was dressed in a sharp suit, dark green, white hair slicked back, a dark cane with a silver knob in one hand. He looked around, smiled at the room in general, and then slowly made his way to the counter.

Olivia reluctantly got up—Peggy was wiping down tables in the back. She stood and watched as the man made his way ever so slowly across the room. *Swish, clunk. Swish, clunk.* Olivia started tapping her fingers on the back of her phone, just for something to do while she waited for him to get to the counter. God, if she ever got that old, she'd just drive her car into a tree.

After what felt like forever, he finally made it to the counter.

"Good morning!" he said, smiling up at her. "My, you're a tall one, aren't you!"

Olivia gripped the counter, hard. He wasn't the first old person to say something like that, but it always grated. Why did old people feel like it was ok to just say whatever flitted through their addled brains?

"What do you want?" she said.

He frowned a bit at her curtness, but tried again with a friendly approach. "I don't know, what's your specialty?"

Olivia gripped the counter, resisting the temptation to grab the man's cane and do something violent with it. She smiled through her teeth. "Coffee. It's a coffee shop. Coffee is our specialty."

He laughed at that, thinking she was making a joke. "Ok, fine, I'll have a small coffee." He looked at the pastry display case. "And one of those muffins. And two of those scones?" He grinned at her. "I'm buying breakfast for my family. I'm visiting them this week."

She didn't respond but proceeded to gather the pastries. She put them in a bag, and then set the coffee cup next to them on the counter. "Coffee is behind you, self-serve. That'll be $21.50."

The man looked shocked. "$21.50? That's a lot."

She shrugged and just looked at him. After a minute, he fumbled in his jacket and pulled out a money clip. His hands shaking, he put two twenties on the counter. Olivia grabbed them, swiftly, glancing around surreptitiously to see if Peggy was around. She wasn't—probably out back having a smoke. Olivia made change . . . but only for thirty dollars, slipping the extra ten under the cash register, to be retrieved later.

"Here you go!" she said, brightly. The man gathered up the pastries, his coffee, and his change, fumbling a bit to gather it all up. He turned to the self-serve counter and started to put the change back into his clip . . . and stopped. Olivia held her breath. He glanced at the change, and then glanced at her. She smiled at him, attempting an innocent look. It didn't work. He looked to open his mouth to speak when the front door opened and a young couple came in. He shook his head and put the change away.

Olivia cashed out the couple while the old man made his coffee. The young couple moved around him to serve themselves politely, and exchanged pleasantries with him. All three left around the same time, the young woman holding the door open for the old man as they exited. Standing at the door, the old man in the green suit looked back at Olivia. "You're not a happy person, are you?" he said to her, in an undertone, and then joined the young couple and left.

Olivia almost didn't hear him, she had been in the process of slipping the ten bucks she had hidden under the cash register into the back of her phone case—all the while keeping an eye out for Peggy. The whisper stopped her in her tracks. She started to go after the man, watching him walk away through the windows at the front of the store. But then another customer came through the front door and Peggy emerged from the back, her smoke break over, and the old man disappeared from sight.

"Where are you going?" Peggy asked, suspicious.

Olivia cursed to herself as she returned, without a word, to the counter, and looked at the new customer.

"What do you want?"

***

Olivia sat on the floor of her room, leaning against her bed, scrolling on her phone. She was hiding from the world, but also, specifically, the group of women that her mom had assembled in the living room to look at her jewelry. It was always a mixed bag when mom had her "shows" at home—on the one hand, the living room never looked so good. On the other hand, Olivia's room was now full of all the detritus that used to be in the living room. She could not WAIT to move out.

She sighed, got up, and started picking up the junk that her mom had thrown into her room, sorting them into piles to make them easier to put away later. Her sister's dirty clothes and shoes—gross—one pile. Old and empty bags of fast food contain-ers, another pile. Random box? It had a bunch of handwritten labels on the outside: Kitchen Dishes—Fragile, Winter Hats, Art Supplies. All of them were crossed out. She opened up the box. It had an assortment of random things: a fedora hat from a costume, postcards from all over the world, some paperback novels—authors she had never heard of, an old Lego Star Wars set and some vintage figurines. Cassettes and CDs—bands she knew her mom hated, Van Halen, Rush. Old pictures, the kind you print out, some black and white, some color. She flipped through them, finding old photos of her parents, laughing, happy. Snapshots of her dad in his army uniform in front of the Eiffel Tower with a bunch of other guys in uniform. A program for his funeral, some random bible verse on the front.

Underneath it all, an old passport. "Oliver Grayson." Her dad, and her namesake. She looked at the picture and smiled. He had a lopsided handsomeness that seemed to fit his face and his personality. She flipped through the rest of the pages, noting stamps from all over the world—France, Germany, Japan, Australia. Places she would never see.

Sighing, she set the passport aside and carefully put everything back into the box. She found a safe place for it in her room, at the top of her closet, away from the havoc of her mom and sister. She took one last look at the passport and then tucked it into her pocket. She WOULD get out of this town. She WOULD see the world.

***

"Excuse me?"

Olvia looked up from her phone to find someone had entered and made it all the way to the counter with out her noticing. Oh, shit, it was Kaylee, perfect Kaylee. Kaylee had been in a couple of times, and Olivia had stalked her online—not that it was hard. Kaylee was an influencer, posting videos every day about her hair, her makeup, her workout routine. Today, she was dressed in a sundress—flowing and shimmering and light green, looking like the sun shining through spring leaves. The fabric seemed almost alive in the way the light played on the contours of the material. Olivia looked around, but Peggy was nowhere to be seen. Olivia got up, walked to the cash register, attempted to paste a smile on her face, hated herself immediately for doing it. She wanted to hate Kaylee just like she hated all of the other customers, but she was so perfect, so everything that Olivia wanted to be.

"Can I help you?"

Kaylee smiled at her, a wide smile with perfect, evenly-spaced teeth. "Hello! You were here the other day, weren't you?"

Olivia blinked. Yes. Of course she was; she was here every day. People were so . . . whatever. She forced a smile.

"Yes, I was. How can I help you?"

Kaylee's smile faltered, then came back, almost like it was plastered on her face. "Oh. Pumpkin spice latte, please."

Olivia almost laughed in her face. Of course, OF COURSE the first pumpkin spice latte of the fall would be from someone this basic.

Kaylee paid, and Olivia busied herself making the drink. After being busy all morning, the shop was eerily quiet now. And where was Peggy anyway? Kaylee watched her make the drink, which was a bit odd? She turned around and put the drink on the counter with a little too much force, almost spilling it.

"Here you go, one pumpkin spice latte."

Kaylee smiled at her. "Thanks." She didn't move and just looked at Olivia. Olivia held her stare for a minute and then looked away and shuffled to the espresso machine, grabbing a rag to clean it, anything to avoid her gaze.

"Can I ask you a question?"

Olvia stopped wiping down the equipment and turned to look across the counter.

"Uhh . . . sure?"

Kaylee cocked her head, her perfect hair shifting with her, falling attractively to one side. "Are you happy?"

Olivia stared at Kaylee, really looking at her. She seemed—perfect. Too perfect. Most influencers used filters to look the part, but Kaylee looked like she had never needed a filter in her life. Medium height, slim but not too skinny, not too tall but not too short, either. Manicured fingernails. Sandals that had just a little bit of heel, enough to be stylish and pretty but not over the top. Green, piercing eyes peeking out from under blonde bangs, blinking at her, open and empty of any emotion except a benign curiosity.

Kaylee was still looking directly at her, expectant, waiting for an answer to her question. Olivia blinked. "Excuse me?"

"You seem not to be happy with yourself."

"I'm fine."

Slowly, like she was approaching a shy animal, Kaylee reached out with both hands and took Olivia's hand in hers. Olivia was so surprised, she didn't react. A spark, green and filled with an energy Olivia had never felt before, jumped from the woman's hand to Olivia.

"I can help you, if you want, " Kaylee said.

Olivia felt warm and cold at the same time. Her mouth tasted suddenly like the stuff her mom used to give her when she had a cold and needed to sleep—sharp, astringent, bitter. Olivia tried to pull back, but Kaylee held fast.

"Look. Look." Kaylee gestured to the phone in Olivia's hand. Olivia lifted it and triggered the camera with her thumb. She gasped.

She was . . . shorter, her hair less curly, her back straight, her pimples gone. Her lashes were longer and her hair was . . . blonde? She looked like . . . who did she look like? Not herself.

Kaylee released her hand, and the energy drained away. Olivia watched her appearance change, almost like a SnapChat filter, back to her old, normal, less glamorous self.

Kaylee turned away and busied herself at the condiments counter, putting even more sugar into her pumpkin spice latte. The room, which had seemed empty of noise before, returned to normal, and Peggy bustled out of the back store room while a group of high school boys burst through the front door. It was eerie the way the people and noise burst into the room—almost like someone or something had been holding them back, keeping them from happening. Before Olivia could react, the high school boys were at the counter, and Kaylee was at the door. She turned to Olivia and spoke, but Olivia was convinced that she spoke only to her, that no one else in the room could hear.

"Don't you want to be happy?"

And with that, she slipped out of the store. The door slammed. One of the high school boys burped, loudly, making the rest of them laugh and slap him on the back.

***

Olivia was at home, in her room, flat on her back on her bed, staring blankly at the glow-in-the-dark stars her mom had put on her ceiling. She couldn't stop thinking about that afternoon, holding hands with Kaylee, the quietness in the shop.

"Olivia! Food!!" Her mom called from the other room. Olivia didn't move. She tried to remember exactly what she looked like when that green spark had flowed through her. Did she look like herself, but just . . . better? No. She was . . . transformed, somehow.

Changed into someone else completely. Did she want that?

She sighed and reached for the money in her pocket. She had still managed to skim some money today. She grabbed the box of things left over from her father and tucked the passport and the cash in the box. She was just sliding the box back into the hiding spot in her closet when the door to her room slammed open. Startled, Olivia spun around, closing the closet door behind her. Her sister stood at the door, her posture slumped, a sly look on her face. "What was that?"

Olivia strode over to slam the door in her sister's face. "KNOCK. FIRST. YOU. ASSHOLE." Her sister slid into the room, sidestepping Olivia neatly in a way that belied her size and demeanor.

"Whatever. Mom says come eat. She made dinner."

Olivia started to yell at her sister to get out but hesitated, the meaning behind her sister's mumbled sentence finally making it to her brain. "Mom made dinner?"

Her sister grunted in what might have been a chuckle, Olivia wasn't quite sure. "Yeah. It's going to be bad, huh, huh, huh," her sister chortled.

"Girls! Come eat!"

Olivia's sister shuffled out of her room and down the hall, toward the kitchen where they ate because the dining room table was always too cluttered. Olivia, still a bit shocked that her mother was actually making dinner, followed, carefully closing the door behind her.

The kitchen was in a state of complete disaster, even more than it normally was. Pots and bowls and wooden spoons, all covered in various sauces and batters, were strewn everywhere. A bag of flour, still half full, lay in the middle of the floor, flour spilling all around it. Smoke wafted from a pan on the stove, smelling of something sour and rotten and fishy.

"Remember when we went to the city and ate at that Korean restaurant?" Her mother looked at them with her normal sense of oblivious cheeriness. "Olivia, you really liked it, and I felt so bad about, you know, what happened, so I decided to try to make Kimchi! With some fish on the side. Here, take a plate."

Amid the mayhem, her mother had cleared a space on the counter and had filled three plates with a mysterious slimy mix of vegetables, a red sauce of some sort, and fish fillets that looked both burned and undercooked.

Her sister lumbered over and sniffed the plate. "Gross," she said, but still took it and started picking at the food.

Her mother slapped her sister on the shoulder. "Wait, c'mon, let's eat in the dining room like civilized people. " She grabbed Olivia's plate and nudged her sister forward with her shoulder. "C'mon, Olivia!"

The dining room was normally given over to her mom's jewelry "business"—and still was, but the table was clear—perhaps for the first time Olivia could remember. There was a small eagle in the middle of the table made of inlaid wood—she couldn't remember ever seeing that in her life. The small boxes and tools and brushes and wire that normally covered the table were stacked precariously in the corners of the room and on the sideboard. Her sister brushed against a stack and it fell, spilling small beads, red, blue and white, all across the floor.

Her sister stopped and looked at the mess she had made, but her mom just shrugged. "It's ok. We'll clean it later. Sit, sit." Her mother sat, putting the plates down on—were those placemats? Where did those come from? Her sister sat and started pawing at her food.

Her mother slapped her on the shoulder again, lightly. "Wait for your sister!"

Olivia was still standing at the doorway, a bit in shock. Her mother waved at her. "C'mon, Olivia. Come sit with us."

Olivia took in the scene. Her mother, covered in flour, her hair sticking up in bits and pieces all over the place, looking at her expectantly. Her sister, wearing yesterday's t-shirt still, shoulders hunched, hands in her lap, looking at her plate. And Olivia just . . . couldn't. It was too much. She didn't want any of this; this was not how her life was supposed to be. Without a word, she turned away.

"Olivia?" her mother called after her.

Olivia ran through the wreckage of the kitchen, trying not to sob, grabbing her backpack on the way out the door. She jumped in her car and backed out of the driveway. Her mom appeared in the doorway as she pulled away, yelling something Olivia couldn't hear, didn't want to hear. She turned her music up loud and just drove, not sure where to, other than . . . away.

Hours later, she found herself sitting in her car, finishing the last french fry at the bottom of the paper bag. After her outrage and anger had passed, her stomach had reasserted itself. And here she was, pathetically eating by herself in the parking lot of the park in the nice part of town, watching families prettier and wealthier than hers play and eat and be . . . better than she was. She took a bite of her sodden cheeseburger and chewed, not even tasting the food, just going through the motions to satisfy the hunger in her stomach and her soul. Maybe she was an optimist, forever scrolling through more videos, forever hoping something would click and her life wouldn't be a sucking maw of mediocrity.

And just then—Kaylee walked by. Olivia slunk further down in her seat, trying not to be seen. She was walking hand in hand with—oh my God, it could be her twin, but male? Tall, blonde, thin and fit, broad shoulders. He turned and smiled at Kaylee, his teeth straight and even and white, his bright green eyes twinkling. Of course, of course Kaylee would have a perfect boyfriend. They got into a new brand new Tesla, shiny and green, and pulled out of the parking lot. After a moment's hesitation, and not quite knowing why, Olivia sat up and pulled out after them.

She followed them at a safe distance, not wanting them to see her stalking. It was starting to get dark—the street lights were blinking on, one by one, and there was enough traffic for her to keep them in sight without being completely obvious she was shadowing them. It didn't take long for them to slow down and turn into a gated community. Crap! How was she supposed to make it past the guard? Olivia glanced around her car, looking for a solution—and spotted the leftover bags from her fast food dinner. An idea flashed through her brain. With one hand, she stuffed the remnants of her dinner back into the bag, and made a half-hearted attempt to make it look like it hadn't been opened. She turned into the community driveway and pulled up to the guard shack. The shack was occupied by a young man, dressed in a rent-a-cop uniform, black hair slicked back, perfectly groomed mustache.

She held up the fast-food bag and attempted a friendly smile. "Doordash." He looked at her, at the bag. "For the Coopers?"

She made a show of pretending to look at the receipt on the

bag, hoping he couldn't read it from where he was. "Yeah."

He waved her on, clicking a button to lift the barrier gate. She held her breath and drove through, watching the guard in her rearview. He was already looking at his phone, watching a video of something she couldn't quite see. Now . . . where to find Kaylee? She accelerated and took the first turn randomly, hoping for a glimpse of—there! She spotted the tail lights of the green Tesla parked in front of a nice duplex. Olivia turned and parked behind a large truck on the street, watching the two beautiful people get out of the car, hoping they hadn't seen her pull into the street.

She watched, hoping that there was something she could hate about them. The beautiful boy that was with Kaylee stopped at the door, and they kissed. Olivia could feel her cheeks heating up. Was she jealous? Embarrassed? Maybe something else? She wasn't sure. He turned to leave, and Kaylee stood, watching and waving as he got into his Tesla and drove away. Olivia slunk down into her seat as he drove past.

After he was gone, she stared at Kaylee's door. This. This life. She wanted this. The beautiful boyfriend, the beautiful car, the beautiful life. If Kaylee could give it to her, she was all in. Olivia brushed the french fry crumbs off her shirt and quickly looked in the mirror, adjusting her hair. Then she took a deep breath and got out of the car. Looking up and down the street, she walked up to the front door and knocked. Kaylee answered the door a few minutes later, a surprised look on her face.

"I want in," Olivia said, without preamble. "Whatever it is, whatever you want, I'll do it, I just—I can't be me anymore."

Kaylee stared at her for a moment, and then opened the door a bit wider. "Follow me," she said and turned down the hallway.

Olivia did as she was told, trailing behind Kaylee as they made their way through the house, all white tile and stainless steel and open floor plan. She led her out the back of the house through a sliding glass door to the backyard. In the back corner of the yard was a small wooden shed, painted a mottled green, with neat rows of flowers growing in front of it, and moss starting to cover the roof. It looked and felt very out of place. Kaylee opened the door and went in. Olivia hesitated for a minute—what was she getting herself into? This shed was weird. But then again, this whole thing was weird. She had to do this. She had to change. She had to leave her old life behind. She ducked down and entered the shed.

Inside, it smelled earthy, but not in an unpleasant way. It reminded her of the way it smelled right after it rained. The room was warm, but Olivia couldn't quite figure out why, the chill from the night air outside gone. Kaylee was busy lighting candles, going from corner to corner in the shed, lighting one candle in each, and muttering under her breath as she did so. The shed seemed bigger on the inside than was possible. One wall held up a rickety old shelf lined with pots and small shovels and bags of seeds. In the other corner, a small gardening table stood underneath a small window. The window looked out the back of the shed and seemed to frame the mountains beyond, silhouetted against the moonlit sky. Standing and looking out the window, it almost felt like she was in a cottage in the woods.

Together, with Kaylee wordlessly instructing Olivia, they cleared a space on the dirt floor in the middle of the structure. Kaylee pulled out a series of stones from a bottom shelf and laid them on the floor in a small ring. Olivia watched as Kaylee continued to work, pulling out kindling and small branches and sticks.

Soon, she had a small fire burning. The smoke drifted up and out of a small hole in the roof that Olivia hadn't noticed before but must have been built for just this type of occasion. Kaylee sat on the floor before the fire, indicating that Olivia do the same. She took Olivia's hand in hers.

"Are you ready?" Kaylee looked into Olivia's eyes, steady and unblinking. Olivia held her gaze, uncomfortable but determined. "Once you do this, you will not be able to go back. Your friends won't recognize you; your family won't know you. You will be forgotten."

Olivia swallowed and nodded. "There's nothing much to remember, anyway."

Kaylee frowned. "We all make ripples, marks in each other's lives. You have family, people who love you, people who know you. They will miss you."

Oliva looked away from those piercing green eyes. She thought of her mom, with her endless hobbies and get-rich schemes. She would be sad—but just like she had done with Olivia's father, her mom would pack her life up in a box and bury it under next week's passion. She thought of her sister—she would just be happy to have Olivia's room and her clothes. She turned back to Kaylee and shook her head.

"They won't. Trust me. " Kaylee raised an eyebrow, concern still written on her face. Olivia straightened up, tried to put a serious tone into her voice. "I'm ready. Please."

Kaylee sighed. "It is your choice." She handed Olivia a small bowl of dried leaves and roots and maybe mushrooms—different shapes and colors, faded reds and yellows and greens. "Put them in the fire."

Kaylee had an identical bowl, and together, they tossed the contents of their bowls into the fire. The leaves caught fire, burning a bright green, and Kaylee took both of Olivia's hands as the smoke filled the room.

Olivia felt the urge to cough, but Kaylee squeezed her hand. "Breathe," Kaylee whispered, and Olivia did, the smoke now so thick she could barely see. "Close your eyes. Breathe."

Olivia closed her eyes and inhaled. The smoke was sweet and didn't burn her lungs. She opened her eyes, and the smoke had started to glow all around them, burning with the same spark that Kaylee had passed to her in the coffee shop, but brighter, more vibrant. She inhaled again and felt rather than saw the green suffuse her entire body with energy. Her body started to change, her limbs contracting. Through the smoke, she could see Kaylee, too, was changing—her face changing to the old man with the cane, and then the muumuu woman, and to another face, and another, faces Olivia didn't recognize.

But something was wrong. It didn't stop, like before. She kept getting smaller and smaller, the room getting big around her. She tried to get up, to move away from the fire, but Kaylee held fast, and the smoke, the green energy, seemed to tie them together, seemed to move now FROM Olivia back to Kaylee. It changed color, going now from green to purple, and Kaylee felt herself falling even further, the shelves now towering above her like small buildings, the stones of the fire ring like boulders dropped by giants.

Finally, the smoke was gone, and Olivia lay sideways on the floor, unable to move her hands or feet. Olivia tried to scream, to yell at Kaylee—who had obviously screwed things up—to do it again, to make her beautiful like she was in the coffee shop before. But she found her face was—frozen. Her entire body was paralyzed except her eyes. She began to panic but couldn't move, couldn't speak, could only shift her eyes back and forth, desperate to communicate.

Kaylee, back to her original form, stood, reached down, and lifted Olivia off the ground like a doll. Carefully, she carried her out of the shed and back into the house. Olivia tried screaming, tried moving, but was still completely immobile. Kaylee padded up the marble steps to the second floor and opened a door off the hallway—a room that could have been a small office or a walk in closet. White shelves lined one half of the room, and a full-length mirror lined the other half. The shelves contained dolls, dozens of them, male, female, young, old, all molded, shaped to be the most perfect tiny version of themselves. Kaylee lifted Olivia and held her close to the mirror. If Olivia could have, she would have gasped—she was tiny, maybe ten inches tall, but beautiful, her hair perfect, her skin flawless, her eyes the same color as before but so bright they almost glowed.

"I've shifted you," Kaylee said. "You wanted to be something else. I've made you the most perfect version of you. Aren't you happier now?"

Olivia looked at Kaylee and noticed she was—younger? Her hair, while beautiful before, shone in the light. Residual whisps of green energy clung to her. She stood just a hair taller, back straighter, teeth whiter, nose perkier. That BITCH. This was for HER. Olivia struggled to lash out, to yell, to move, anything . . . but couldn't.

"There, there," Kaylee said. "You'll get used to this soon. And look, you're not alone. " Kaylee lifted the new Olivia to the shelf and placed her next to a young man whose eyes followed the two of them with a hatred that mirrored Olivia's rage. "Enjoy your new home and your new form. I told you I could help you. I gave you what you said you wanted, what you all said you wanted." She swept the room with her gaze, smiling beatifically—and then turned and closed the door on Olivia and the rest of the shifted, all of whom could do nothing but stare at themselves and each other.

YOUR BLOOD WILL FUEL OUR MACHINES

Keegan Young

Two hours ago, Jms was schmoozing it up at a corporate party. Now, he's crawling through air return ducts and access panels. After more Crystal Pepsi champagne than his detox chip (alcinhib) can handle and plasticking smiles while empty-air chattering with corporate tools, crawling up dark and dusty shafts is a reprieve.

Frett all that, he thinks. *There are quicker ways to corporate gold.*

It'd been a simple matter to excuse himself for the restroom and slip up the ceiling panels. His smart.suit switched from the expensive-looking Dujani over to cloak.mode, became slim, dark, light-absorbing, and the shoes shrank to flexi.supergrip sound-absorbing footwear. The gathering's well after work hours on a central floor, so the building is cleared out. Only the occasional jani.tor drones traverse the halls. The security systems have an easily-accessible backdoor, and his implants can mimic the same signal the cleaning drones gave off, so they think he's one of them. Fairly straightforward.

Next, it's just gaining access to the server floor.

Jms' iWallet deconstructs into tools to undo the air vent grate. He doesn't worry about getting it back in place. Leaves it sitting on the floor unscrewed. When he's done, the company will have bigger issues to worry about. If they survive a week.

Jms only has to crawl through a bit of venting and two levels of ceiling space. He isn't claustrophobic, but what initially seems like a short, comfortable vent transforms into a very tight tunnel that stretches out impossibly before him. Situations like these are why he doesn't use Bioshaping for a muscular form. He needs to be hale but slim enough to fit in these spaces—which he barely does.

Jms concentrates on breathing, echoing loudly off the duct walls, right in his ears. Elbows work more than hands or whole arms can within the limited space. Feet can only inch him a bit forward, not enough space to bend his knees. His Health screen pops up on his retina, noting his elevated heart rate and blood pressure, which he's well aware of. It's the same notification for his adrenaline-fueled hyperfocus, warning when he's risking adrenal toxicity. He focuses on breathing and moving forward. Finally, he reaches the exit panel. He pops it off and slides out.

He takes a big breath.

Right, piece of cake.

There's a security door, but he hacks it in two mins. The server room is ice-cold and breezy, blue-lit from various glowing and flickering server/router lights. This place has its own security systems and drones, but they all fell under the spell of his Screenmate4000 (SM4K). The cybersecurity AI assistant is essential for corporate espionage.

He finds the right 7' server tower towards the back and plugs in a small cartridge. A tiny LED lights. Jms blinks and looks left, accessing his digi-eye screen. It confirms his operator team is connected and working on gaining entry. Jms has a programming team, remote and ready at all times. Then he waits.

He glances around. Checks his internal screen again.

Something's wrong.

It's connected, but it isn't getting anywhere with the server.

He double-checks things on his end, makes sure the server's network connections are intact, observes the cartridge's diagnostic. All clear.

Why isn't this working? Jms begins to sweat, despite the cold.

A crash sounds, loud from the floor below.

"Shigg!" Jms swears, his heart rate jumping. *What the hell's going on?*

***

"So? How'd it get done?" Hns Mann gulps his green mush and smacks his lips loudly.

Jms shrugs, not wanting to get into the meeting dry. He signals to the mobile bar; it scoots over and delivers him a bourbon neat. He's turned his alcinhib off.

"The server was missing several updates, so it stalled for a few moments, nearly shut down. Then it all went through. The loud crash? One of those stupid jan.itors knocked something over. They're so buggy." He sips more, savoring the burn.

Hns Mann's bedroom is the entire top tower floor of MannGo Industries. He wears a self-designed, free-flowing garment, also smart.cloth. In his baby-soft hands, he holds a drink that looks and smells like grass clippings blended with seaweed and is probably obscenely healthy. Hns drinks a minimum of three a day, at scheduled times. When asked how they taste, he scoffs, saying, "Why's it need to taste good?"

Taste is a strange thing indeed. His bedroom is 30x30 ft, permaglass smart windows with auto-adjusting tint that can broadcast any channel or view at Hns' request. There are no less than six beds of varying shapes, designs, and exotic origins. A bathroom on each corner of the floor, each a different style.

But Hns only has one chair, a form-fitting chairbot that follows him around silently, reading his heart rate, movement, posture, and facial expressions to determine if he wants to sit. Also what seat type he'll want.

With only one chair for Hns, guests sit elsewhere. Jms sits on steps leading down to the sleek silver firepit.

While Hns is the CEO and owner/creator of MannGo, Jms is the acquisition specialist. Jms operates on covert missions of competitive intelligence gathering. He's a seeker, a real-time operator, a professional snoop and thief, if the job requires it. Jms isn't part of the Hns Mann fanclub, couldn't care less for his company or vision. But the job pays well. MannGo is one of the top growing businesses worldwide, has been for two decades. So Jms doesn't want for anything. He never will again. He just has to do the occasional secretive mission or dirty job. A small price to pay in this world. Plus, he gets off on the rush of corporate theft.

"Huh." Hns sits without looking, the bot chair there and forming instantly to the desired incline. He sips more green gunk, chewing occasionally. His eyes lose the far-away look, refocus briefly on Jms. "Well fine, other matters." His smooth, round face brightens into a cherubic smile. "New mission. Objective: Find this." He gestures, electronic dings sound, notifying Jms he has new msgs. Hns often expects everyone else to be on his frequency, just understanding instantly what he's talking/thinking about. Along with assuming everyone else is always connected to their screens, despite him not being connected. Hns only views things on external screens, so it won't interrupt his "genius vision." Real quote.

Jms holds out a few moments, to see if Hns will just explain it anyway. He sometimes does. But Hns continues to stare at him expectantly, so Jms turns an eye roll into a blink and accesses his screen. His eye's still scratchy, probably from climbing through dusty ducts. He reads the recent mail from Hns, sees long lists of reports, corporate, commercial, some intelligence, other things. He skims, because Hns is fidgeting like he's about to talk.

Sure enough, Hns clears his throat. "There's been talk about this lately; think it could really help with my next few projects. Energy's really becoming a problem, and renewable's just not paying off what it promised."

Not paying off what you'd promised, Jms thinks. And many others, with all the sustainable energy projects over the years. The windmill fields and waterways, solar panel roofs, geothermal pits. He wonders where Hns' 'space energy collection' project had gone. Hns had this great idea of collecting unfiltered solar energy and space radiation but stumbled over how to get it planetside. Hns often went on tangents like this, then just moved on. Brilliant genius syndrome.

Jms is losing the thread.

Hns is right. Renewable energy isn't getting back the return in investment and infrastructure building cost. Upkeep and repair isn't so bad, but updating solar panels every few years is too costly. Plus the metals needed are scarcer and scarcer. Not to mention urban solar rarely paid off for those not directly below the skyline. Only skyscrapers benefitted from solar nowadays, being above the haze.

"If we could just get a big push, a payload of cheap energy, I could jump my next projects up, won't hold me back anymore . . ." Hns drops into silent contemplation, chewing more green mush.

Jms sips, waits a few moments. He clears his throat, reminding Hns he's still present. "Uh . . . what's everyone talking about?"

Hns looks about, jowls bouncing, lost for a moment. Having to backtrack or 'slow down' for other people always gives him that confused baby look. Then he snaps his fingers and gestures at a wall screen. He queues up a video combining all the reports he'd just sent, important bits featured. It's faster than most can read, but Jms' SM4K auto-catches the highlighted portions, compiling a list for him to read at his leisure.

Finally, Jms sees. "Cache of oil? I thought all major oil sources had been drained."

"Thought so, too. Scouring deep interest trade webs for the past months, I found this."

"Who the hell has any oil left?"

"That's what I need you to find out."

Jms sighs. "Ok. I assume you've got a list of where I'm to start?"

Hns gestures again. Another electronic jingle sounds in Jms' head; another msg.

"Right," Jms says, stowing his annoyance. "If that's all then . . ."

But Hns isn't paying attention. He's turned a different window screen on, showing a nature doc, an old one, about superstorms and river/coastal flooding. Strange that he always watches that.

Jms knocks back his drink and leaves.

***

Jms arrives at his place in the BellEdison biocon later that afternoon. He has the rest of the day off after reporting on his mission. He's more often on particular assignments every few days rather than the usual 48 hours on-call business schedule. The assignments might be more difficult and dangerous on occasion, but it beats a daily grind. He's done his time with that.

His biocon suite has two floors and several rooms. Not huge, but just right for him. An entryway and living area, kitchen and bathroom downstairs; upstairs, his bedroom, a study/office, and his reflection room, as he calls it, with its plants and an unfiltered window. He often spends his time in this last room late at night, his phone and screens off, just drinking and staring at the buildings above the clouds, the airrides drifting about, and beacon lights for traffic lanes. From this view, everything looks far away, a world apart. He'll just stare and lose himself in thought and drink until he's numb all over, can barely keep his eyes open and can *almost* stop wondering about if he hadn't been left behind.

His bioparents were caught up in the 'Reclaim the Earth' wave, the early 2100s enviro-movement. Sick of watching states and companies pollute and destroy the earth, people got together to start radical conservation efforts: buying up land and isolated islands, starting communes, and aggressive natural reclamation projects. Some of it was mostly legal, like shutting down major polluting factories regardless of the jobs lost or workers displaced. Some (the unpublic bits) bordered on ecoterrorism, like causing several landslides/avalanches that wiped out popular elite resorts. But many who joined up with the 'Reclaimers' left families/kids behind, especially those that did the morally questionable stuff. They said they had to save the world or else there'd be nothing left for their kids and grandkids. The idea was they'd eventually return. But many got so caught up in the work, they never did. Always more work to be done, more Earth to save.

Jms was of the 'Unclaimed.' Had no idea who his bioparents were; he was just on record as having parents in the 'Reclaimers Corp.' Supposedly this record is on file in the state Fostercare system, but he'd never had to access it. They held back all info about his actual family to deter running. If family wants to visit, they have to make contact, fill out all forms within a certain time. Once family's in the visitors system, it's easier to keep visiting. So it hurt twice as bad when no one ever bothered.

As much as his efficient, secure, well-stocked and self-cleaning suite is the epitome of modern living in the US Sector, it doesn't completely wipe away his past. He can surround himself with corporate employee accessories, but he can't forget the dirty streets he grew up in, especially the Fostercare Center, the place they stayed in between fosterhomes. Though he wanted to be forgotten by them and the system.

Or so Jms thought. But someone *had* been keeping tabs on him. After gen-ed., while doing workforce training to satisfy probation, he was actually doing side jobs with some friends. They were hijacking delivery drones and reselling the packages. It was a local small delivery company; they hadn't thought anyone would notice a few lost deliveries.

Someone took notice.

They'd been on a rooftop in the lower haze, in between HVAC units, dissembling drones. They'd jammed their signals then had overridden their code to land. They were reprogramming them for their own personal network.

That Someone showed up in a personal, sparkling blue skyster, a silvery, natural silk-spun suit, and an impeccable haircut. Hns Mann, with gleaming Dior mirrorshades reading all their iDents and data, stared straight at Jms.

"You."

An accomplice tried to play it off—"Hey man, we're not doing anything wrong,"—though he was surrounded by repurposed drone guts.

Hns ignored him, continued pointing with his mirrorshades at Jms. "Your talents are wasted here."

Jms raised an eyebrow. "What else am I 'sposed to do?"

Hns said, "This is so small. You could be bigger. Work for me. I'll show you."

This was when Jms' accomplices started saying how helpful they could be. Hns cut them off. "Please, you are competition I crush daily."

So Jms went with him; he had nothing to lose. For years, he trained in cutting edge "requisition of operational information or properties for economic/commercial purposes." He learned how to look and sound professional, how to blend in at corporate parties, how to move in the economic world. But especially how to be the best thief in the business.

And yet, the info about his parents is still locked up in the Fostercare database. He could probably obtain it easily now. But he no longer cares. The wound of wondering who his family is had long since scarred over.

What does he need family for? Especially the kind that abandons you.

Jms goes for another drink, his eyes drifting to the red-light district, neon animations of exotically dressed folk dancing enticingly.

Suddenly turned on, Jms gives the command to his SM4K, though it's already reading his pulse and brain waves and preparing his special bed. The Purple-Siemens Skinmaster 5X bed is extending out of its wall compartment when he arrives in his bedroom. He disrobes and lays down as a VR goggle set is placed on his head.

The instructions for this special Amor(ph)ous bed advise never to use it without the goggles accessory, or at least a blindfold. Just like the Wizard of Oz, seeing behind the curtain ruins the illusion. After that, it's hard to go back. Jms knows without the goggles, the bed produces a number of mechanical arms and attachments, the most recognizable being a round hip-shaped device with wet mech-mouths mimicking the human (or animal) vagina and anus. The rest are just bizarre appendages disturbing to see out of context. Jms has a program for the bed to complete his fantasy. It suits his purposes. He doesn't connect well with people, and dating's too much work. He doesn't need to rely on anyone for this.

He's immersed in a dark candlelit bedroom of classical opulence, a gigantic bed with thick, soft comforters and dozens of pillows. Jms lays down in the center on his back. Out of the shadows steps a vision of voluptuous beauty, shimmering transparent silk hugging her curvaceous body as she walks towards him, her full, glossy lips catching the light. The cloth falling away to reveal gleaming, soft skin. She climbs atop him, her weight pressing down on him at the hips, then her hands reach out to caress his chest, shoulders, and biceps. He's hard and ready beneath her, his hips thrusting up a little, but she pulls up and away, teasing him, before finally pressing her weight again on him. Then she slides him inside herself, warm and wet, as he gasps out loud. She slowly rides him, hips rising and falling, grinding against him in that angle he loves, slowly for a bit, occasionally slowing or stopping, then coming back down and picking up the pace. Her hands grip where his arms and shoulders meet, pushing him down into the bed, while her breasts and hair graze his chest, her moist mouth nibbling at his neck and chin and ear. Jms begins thrusting up into her, his hips bucking, wild with desire. The rhythm drives harder and faster, her voice moaning into his neck and ear, breath hot, until he finishes. They lay there shuddering for several moments. She climbs off him and bends down to gently lick him clean.

In the orgasmic aftermath, Jms can feel how synthetic everything is. The program does the job, but the results are just OK. Better than the fumbling, awkward sex of his youth. But he's just as empty as before. Maybe he didn't drink enough. In this way, Jms falls asleep.

***

Jms wakes up tangled in his silk sheets with a slight hangover. He turns his alcinhib on, then remembers it doesn't cure hangovers. He takes a detox pill while he waits for his 'presso. His eye twitches left out of habit and brings up his screen, notifications, new mail. From Hns, of course: his next task. Rubbing his temples as his eyes strain to focus on the text, he switches it to audio and downs some water. SM4K hums in his head, forming words in his mind with no conscious effort on his part.

"Morning. Next mission: CardinalZero is preparing for a big buy. Lunch in NeoHaven today for potential buyers/traders. Infiltrate. They'll have some info on this oil cache."

Jms doubts he'll find any oil cache; there aren't any big reserves left. This is just another lost cause. He'll be chasing whispers of ghosts of traces of . . . something. But whatever; it matters to Hns. Jms gets paid no matter what. When Jms comes back empty-handed after buying off, bankrupting, or sabotaging other companies, Hns might throw a little tantrum then move on to something else. Some other pet genius project. Nevermind all the jobs lost or financial ruin caused.

Whatever. Not Jms' problem.

Hangover gone, Jms drains his coffee and gets dressed. He adjusts his smart.suit to look nice and expensive, sleek dark colours, a different design from the last party.

***

The lunch is predictable. Cybersuits configured to a sheen, prosthetic grins all around. Bioshaped perfectly muscular and/or voluptuous forms in custom-designed fashion, smiling suggestively behind drinks or firing veiled barbs barely disguised behind business chatter. The drinks are OK, the food's decent. But it's all the same. Jms participates in the absolute minimum conversation, trying to sequester those with the most power. How sharp the haircut is matters, judging by the razor-cut hairstyles he sees the corporate reps sporting.

Jms remembers in his teens in Fostercare, some of the kids got into cutting hair. Counselors forced them to get jobs, to somehow form them into 'functional society members,' so it was better to choose what you liked. Cutting hair was popular on the street. And they got good at it. Not all the robots in the world could give a precision cut like one of the homeys. Jms never had the knack himself, but he respected it, respected the hustle.

The human-made cuts always look better.

Jms is intellectually-pirating a higher-up circle, getting tidbits in between club and drug talk, when he sees something in his periphery. His enhanced vision picks up a face, boosts up the quality and links it to some files in his data stores.

Without turning his head, he focuses on the image painted on his retina. He recognizes the person. His heart rate increases.

Yna Hopper.

Yna is an old rival from the Fostercare years. Yna's taller than the average female-oriented person, taller than him now (Jms isn't sure if this is biogen or not). Now, she's really filled out, sharp little mouth, blonde hair in a graduated bob, playful but serious glint to her purple eyes. She's making a show of tucking the longer bits behind her ear, harmless flirting to draw potential victims in. Yna Hopper, in the mix with the other suits sipping Cocoa Puffs liquor, acting fascinated so she could no doubt move up the corporate chain faster.

Jms and Yna had never been friends nor enemies exactly. More like social rivals. Anytime Jms would be hustling for a living, trying to keep space for himself, Yna would suddenly be nearby, doing the same thing better, easier, and with that stupid grin on her face, as if to say, "See how little work I do to achieve the same results as you?" It always irked Jms.

Yna did this back in Fostercare, too. Once she realized she

didn't have to fight like mad to stay on top, that she could just vamp to get what she wanted, it changed the game. Even just some small banter, and she'd be gelling with the counselors and potential fosterparents. She cried abuse to the right people to get out of nasty homes and into better ones, and moved on up until she landed in some rich fuck's home, some multi-billionaire owner of a line of tenhabs, and after that, Jms never saw her again. She'd maneuvered her way into a better life.

It bothered Jms, because he'd been doing the same thing: flirting, manipulating. Only Yna did it effortlessly. That'd aggravated him to no end.

Now she's here, all grown up and mixing with corpo-crowds. *What's her angle?* Jms wonders.

Not exactly a heartwarming reunion.

She glances his way, but her smile and conversation doesn't miss a beat. How practiced, and these corporate rats are falling for it.

Jms moves so Yna's not in sight anymore as he chats with other folks, but his focus is shot. Luckily smart.chat logs conversations he can hear and gives him a rundown when he asks. Still, he wonders, *What the hell's Yna's game?*

Now, she's grinning again as she chops it up with these other execs and meddlers, most of which Jms' pegged as pretty but powerless. Why's she wasting time with them?

Jms needs a drink. He shuts off his alcinhib and orders a double vodka tonic from the autobar. Synthetic vodka tastes awful, but enough of it does the job. The sharp taste clears his mind, until he notices a presence to his left. He turns his head enough so the peripheral sensors pick up the image, match it in his memory—it's

Yna. Probably come to gloat.

"Can I help you?" he says, turning smoothly to Yna. Up close, she's even prettier than he remembers. A hot corporate foil in a body-hugging suit, all organic threads. He scoffs. *So that's where her tastes have led.*

Yna ignores his question and orders a drink, her lips curving playfully. Her dry martini arrives, she drinks it in one smooth swallow, leaving the olive. She gives a moue of disgust. "Ugh, they could've gotten real booze at least. But enough will do the job." Her smile turns on full-blast.

Jms' eyebrow twitches. "What d'you want?" he says, ordering another drink against SM4K's advice.

"Hi, how've you been all these years? Nice to see you survived."

"Clearly, you've done very well for yourself. Great, wonderful, congrats. What're you doing here?"

Her smile hardens.

"You're after it, too, aren't you? The big cache?" Yna's purple eyes flash.

Jms' face is machine solid, but his eyes twitch left, checking to see if his data has been hacked. "I don't know what you mean," he says, sipping his second drink. It's slightly less terrible than the first.

"Everyone here's hunting. Some don't know exactly what 'it' is, but their bosses have them sniffing the trail. It's led here." She glances over at him. "Not surprised to find you. You always knew how to find things, work people. I knew immediately; you're after it, too."

"Still don't know what you're talking about," Jms says with a suddenly empty drink in hand. *Oops.* He turns his alcinhib on now, so it'll catch some alcohol entering his bloodstream, strip it down into harmless sugars.

"Fine, be that way. But if you change your mind, want to go over notes, maybe collaborate later, let me know." She gives him a sly look as she returns her glass to the autobar. Jms walks angrily away.

She wants to 'collaborate.' To use him for more info, skills she's no doubt sharpened over the years as another business shark, gobbling up idiots who fall for a pretty face and shiny leggings. Well, she'll get nothing from him.

There's a clinking of knife on drink glass, and CardinalZero's CEO, Kty Kuhn, begins her speech.

Jms' passive net picks up encrypted emails her subordinate, Tms Carr, sends out. They're all personal invites to another meeting room in 30 minutes. This is where the real deals will happen, what he needs to know!

Jms' SM4K copies an email and personal security code for that meeting room, and he heads there. A few floors up, less busy elevators and hallways. Jms changes his smart.suit to appear more generic, to mimic a style similar to the other suits at the lunch party, blend into an average amalgam. Then he slips into the door of the VIP meeting just behind someone else. Tms Carr looks around and gives a second, uncertain glance to Jms. But Jms stands relaxed and motionless. The best way to fit in is to act like you belong there. The younger man checks a wristscreen and says, "Let's get started."

Nothing starts. More blatherings, more corporate jargon, party niceties—Jms's bored, but this is buttering up for the main course. Jms listens while his peripheral watches the other invitees.

He's dismayed to see Yna there, as well, rubbing elbows with some newly made friends. But Jms keeps to the other side of the room, trying to pick out who could be key in this. He guesses they'll reveal some special offer, and he'll have to isolate the biggest competition and deal with them. Jms is authorized to spend in Mann's stead, but Jms prides himself on alternatives to direct monetary means. He grew up poor and had to find other ways to survive, and he still uses those skills. That's why Mann hired him.

Although some expensive tools help a little.

Out of the several companies present, the biggest rivals are Pear, Civi, MacroHard, CollectedWellness, UnitedTechBusiness (UTB), and AmWorkersFedCreditUnion (AWFCU). Most just have one or two reps, but the smaller companies have more, almost like it'll make up for their smaller market presence. Do they think they can use numbers here to wrangle first dibs on a deal? That's not how this works.

While they all size each other up, Jms' SM4K applies countermeasures into each company's accounts first, as it gains access to more of their systems. At his command, it releases an aggressive virus that corrupts all their data stores, and while their company networks are downed and their wealth-foundations unbalanced, the economic hierarchy is disrupted, and their power here is an empty shell. One by one, he watches them all get the news through their screens and implants, look alarmed, and fall back or even leave the meeting. Tms Carr grows nervous as his potential buyers lose confidence before his eyes.

Yna glances over at Jms, crossing her arms in disapproval. She might suspect him, but she can't stop him. He glances briefly through her company profile with AmGro, but their buying options are too limited and their cyber defenses too strong. He leaves it alone for now.

Tms Carr is sweating visibly. Doubtless, he's reading his internal reports and seeing his options shrink, most competition temporarily waylaid, this secretive meeting now a farce. And Jms is blackmailing through offers before Tms' stupid speech is even over. He'll have this in the bag before long.

Carr finishes weakly, "And . . . so, that concludes our plans for expansion and partnership. So, anyone who's interested, we'll open up the discussion now." A few people, too low level to understand they had been undermined already, approach him, as well as Yna.

Jkb Lorenz of UTB is also there, his large muscular form straining the fabric of his suit, personalized to carry his size and mass of enhancements. He wears a bored expression on his tan, rough, square face. He hasn't reacted to Jms' online maneuvers. And Jkb is cy-enhanced to the gills; there's no way he didn't notice. It worries Jms.

Yna gets there to speak ahead of Jms, but it hardly matters.

Tms' sweating up a storm. Jms walks up to him and smirks, gripping his hand firmly and saying quietly, "I appreciate your business. Good luck and enjoy the hustle." That last bit is what kids would say to each other at Fostercare. It was half jeer and half luck-wishing, an all-purpose phrase. Tms is too shook to comprehend much. Jms goes over to the refreshments table and has a cup of Cherry Kool-Aid brandy.

This'll be a zip, thinks Jms, moments before chaos sets in.

Jkb Lorenz vanished as folks shuffled off in disbelief or whatever, but his re-entrance is quite notable. The conference room door bursts open on the fifty or so people remaining. Jkb charges into the room with six other heavily-armed, heavily-enhanced thug-cygoons. Jkb himself has shed his suit coat, revealing more of his massive, fortified-frame shoulders and arms. One cygoon covers the door.

Everyone freezes. Reading Jms' pulse, SM4K offers Fight or Flight options for adrenal glands and muscle attunement. He twitches his retina, signaling Flight mode. His smart.suit slowly shifts colour and pattern, so he can blend into the wall, just maybe escape notice.

Tms Carr protests, paling visibly. "But—but we don't have any direct hardware here; there's nothing for you to rob."

Jkb nods, thinks, then announces, "That's a lie." To his lackeys, "Clear it out. Take everyone's data."

Then the shooting starts.

The six cygoons start unloading semi-auto guns, targeting people clustered in the medium-sized room. They're using a cross between riot-suppression and military grade, because they fire fast but mostly just incapacitate. Mostly.

Three cygoons fire on attendees, breaking knees and legs before moving further in. Two go to fallen bodies, unconscious or dead, and begin data-retrieval with hardlined brainpan-scanners. The brain-drain device has an invasive spike-claw, which bites into the brainpan so the other insectile parts can forcibly download from cerebral prosthetics. Jkb watches calmly, occasionally stomping legs of competitors feigning injury in an attempt to flee. Some with enhanced legs take much more stomping. Jkb's face is stone cold throughout the screaming.

Some joker has a stun-resist suit and jumps up with a forearm shotgun, emptying all quad barrels into Jkb.

Jkb grunts in surprise. The smoke clears; his shirt is shredded, revealing a titanium-silicon-webbed abdomen, still sparklingly unmarked. Really high-class stuff. Jkb chuckles and draws back a fist, which pistons into the would-be defender. The recipient flies into the wall, denting it, falls down in a pile. Unmoving.

During this initial onslaught, Jms' suit looks like the wall, a vague light blue, and he slides towards a locked door which he furiously goads SM4K to hack. *Faster. Need it open. Now.* Jms sweats. He glances around to see if he's noticed. Spots Yna across the room.

She's frozen against the far wall, cowering with arms up, futilely blocking her from further shot. Her suit shows some damage already, an elasticity shell-lined interior, now fragmentary. A cygoon approaches her, sees her somewhat armored-clothing, pulls out a shock baton.

Yna's fearful expression drops, as do her arms, she braces against the wall.

Her foot blurs out; there's a metal-and-bone crunch.

The thug's knee now bends the other way.

He shrieks, collapses.

SM4K queries several question marks and exclamation points, mirroring Jms' own thoughts. *What the hell kinda enhancement is that?*

Jms notices Tms Carr at a previously concealed backdoor. It's just creaking open when Jms makes his decision. He sets his footgear to zero friction and pushes away from the wall. He glides in between panicked survivors who slip and fall after him as they notice the exit. The doors quickly close on a few grasping hands. Jms turns away from them and pursues Tms down a corridor of degrading lights.

Jms hears a commotion at the door but leaves it behind him. He still needs to know if there's an oil cache.

Jms hits an endless hall, no sign of Tms. He starts a search program on the building specs, then another looking for security access pings from Tms Carr's iDent. The latter gets a response. The wall a few feet behind him shows a footprint, so Jms dives into the security system. Sure enough, there's a concealed door. Jms opens it and slips inside.

Another office space. Barely furnished. Desk. Wallscreen. And packing a suitcase on the desk: Tms Carr. He doesn't notice Jms, so Jms stands there, seeing how far he can get into Tms' data virtually. SM4K shows him the enmeshed code of a tight firewall. *Plan B*, thinks Jms.

Jms walks to the desk Tms messily occupies and leans against it. Tms starts from his reverie but then goes back to his wallscreen. "What? You've already ruined our options. We've got nothing now."

"Not true." Jms casually places his hand a few feet from Tms' suitcase/computer hybrid. He glances at the wallscreen's reflection of the suitcase screen, sees in the lower right corner a program rapidly transferring data. Jms sets his smart.suit to increase malleability at his right armpit. Jms eyes Tms as he hastily stuffs clothes, zip pads, other necessities into the suitcase's regular storage space. "Today's meeting was for a reason. You were making moves to do something big. What is it?"

Tms shakily checks data transfer status while stuffing more things into the suitcase. "Can only tell you that for a price."

Jms slides his hand nearer to the case and shifts his body closer.

He deploys a second skeletal, red right arm, slowly, through the permeable pocket in his smart.suit. This is a cy-attachment, special made. He stretches it out.

Tms turns around again, shoving clothing and toiletries, into the suitcase.

Jms freezes the second right arm, hiding it behind his regular arm.

But Tms is too distracted. He checks the suitcase's top-half screen, types something, then goes back to the wallscreen, gesturing to close out windows of completed programs and transfers.

Jms slides the thin, red arm all the way to the suitcase. It spreads tiny, needle-like fingers, sticking the filament tips into the suitcase, seeking ports. Once connected, Jms begins direct-hacking.

"C'mon, it doesn't matter anymore," Jms says slickly. "You said yourself, your company's done—which, BTW, if it hadn't been me, it would've been anyone else. Everyone's nipping at heels, trying to find out what this big secret is." Jms looks away, the picture of innocence. He makes a show of observing his cuticles, how shiny his nails are.

Tms yanks open a drawer, swigging right from a bottle, brown liquid sloshing around. "No one else would've done it as neatly and quickly as MannGro, that's for sure. Thanks for that. Didn't have to drag this meeting out too long. Well, until fugging Lorenz and UTB crashed things." He laughs humorlessly and drinks again.

Jms chuckles slowly. They're all friends here. He checks his internal screen and watches the percentage slowly creep up. Just a couple more minutes, and he'll have what he needs . . .

Loud crashing noises and shouts ring from elsewhere on the floor. They both look at the doorway. Tms' eyes widen, looking ready to bolt.

Jms waves with his free hand. "Don't worry about it," he drawls comfortingly. "You built this secret path and escape route real well. No one else will find it."

"Pfft. *You* found it."

Jms shrugs. "No one's as good as me."

The noises echo farther away. Tms' shoulders relax a bit. He sips from the bottle, glances down at it, and offers it to Jms.

Unable to shift too much and give away the second red right arm's covert work, Jms leans a bit forward but gestures with his hand, 'slide it this way.' Tms complies, sliding it across the desk. Jms makes a show of drinking, smacking his lips, looking down at the Sprite-Smirnoff Vodka. "Ooh, this is smooth. Not bad for midrange stuff."

Tms searches a cabinet drawer for anything leftover for his nearing escape and glances nervously at the wallscreen upload bar—it's nearly done. Jms checks his eye.screen: 85%.

Tms speaks, "What do you plan to do?"

"What? With this secret cache everyone's hunting for? I dunno. My boss wants it."

Tms pulls an electro-magnum out of the cabinet and aims it at Jms.

Jms freezes. His forced download's at ninety-three percent. *Jesus, just a minute more.*

Tms' voice quivers. "I mean when *they* show up. I've got an escape pod that'll only admit me." A sliding door opens behind him, revealing said pod. It can fit at least three not-too-large people.

"C'mon, there's totally room for me."

"Get your fugging *hands* away from my case."

Shigg, I'm found out.

Jms slowly raises his arms, but not completely disconnecting the red right arm yet, reading ninety-seven percent. "Look, let's talk about-"

BAM.

Jms is knocked head over ass. His chest is paralyzed with pain. He can't breathe.

Luckily, the push.armor held just fine, even at this close range. The small generator shield calculated such a straight-on shot, deflecting and pushing Jms back to expend kinetic energy from the collision. It still hurts like hell and is disorienting as fuck. It'll also take a few minutes to generate energy to deflect another direct shot.

While Jms lies on the ground, trying to keep still while also struggling to breathe fully, he checks his internal screen. The data transfer stopped at ninety-eight percent. Is it enough?

"I saw the flash of your armor. I know you're not dead, but you will be when they get through," Tms calls from the other side of the room. In between shallow breathing, Jms becomes aware of pounding and weaponsfire, *very* close. Just the other side of the wall.

Finally able to draw a full, creaky breath, Jms coughs out, "Just . . . give me . . . something . . ." He rolls over, looking up at Carr.

Tms laughs as something cracks somewhere. "You're almost dead. Whatever. 'Green Futures.' That's all you get."

Jms is working on a msg to Hns when a thud sounds to his left. The door's open already? But it's not. Behind and to his left stands a familiar figure, dirty and tattered clothes hanging off her muscular form. Yna Hopper looks down at him, beaming. "'Green Futures,' huh?"

Jms curses under his still-regaining breath. Tms activates his pod. The doors close, it powers up its small hovermotor and shoots out of the building. A glastene window shows the quickly vanishing pod.

Yna offers her hand to help Jms up. By the further noise, those cygoons will break in any second now, and Jms is better off on his feet. He reluctantly accepts.

"How'd you survive?" wheezes Jms, seeing Yna's deteriorating outfit.

"Ducts."

Jms grunts. The pounding is immense, and the wall's deforming more and more with each sound, bubbling inward. "Think you can handle defending yourself for a bit?"

Yna scoffs, pushing shiny, pale hair behind an ear. "Please. I don't need gadgets to defend myself."

"Yeah, how did you-"

BOOM.

The door explodes inward, and a cygoon collapses with it. Their weapon had apparently detonated. The next cygoon shakes her head and steps over the body into the room, followed by another and Jkb himself.

Autoguns trained on Yna and Jms, Jkb strolls around and takes in the scene. He scans the wallscreen with a device, but the data's corrupt now. He goes to the escape window and taps it, seeing the pod's vapor trails. Turning around, he makes eye contact with his cygoons and jerks a thumb at the window. A woman unslings a large shoulder cannon, which unfolds as she braces herself before the window, boots unlatching spike supports into the floor. She sights through the window at the shrinking dot, the weapon linking in with her own enhanced eye, and pulls the trigger.

FOOMF.

An oblong object pierces the glass as it shoots out. Then a concussive blast rocks the room as the second stage rocket fires. Jms is nearly blown back. Yna had braced herself and puts out a steadying hand to Jms. Jkb stands solid, suit jacket flapping in the wind.

The rocket zips off after the pod. A boom echoes in the distance, above the wind whistling out the ninety-story window.

Jms turns to Jkb and shrugs. "Sorry, I got nothing for you. The . . . *late* Tms Carr refused to give, even in his final moments."

Yna shrugs, too, showing empty hands.

Jkb blinks. "Nice try. You," he says, his metal eyes targeting Jms, "are a sneak. Data-sneaking the whole time. Don't act like you weren't. You got *something*."

Jms shakes his head. "I don't—"

"Stop talking."

More cygoons show up, carrying more guns, swapping out ammo clips or cleaning blood and other fluids off metallic fists.

Yna, taller and more muscular, steps in front of Jms. But Jms puts a hand on her shoulder, not letting her shield him completely. He says, "Listen, Jkb, we still have other options. We—both of us, our companies—have something to offer you. In exchange for our lives."

Jkb cleans clear gunk off the brain-drain. "No," he says, handing the device to another while they all face the two, forming a semicircle. "Done talking."

So that's when Jms and Yna hatch their plan.

When Jkb and the cygoons had first entered the panic room, Yna had sent a msg request to Jms. Actually, she'd sent one earlier at the start of the lunch, back before things got hectic. That msg he'd ignored. This msg was more urgent. Wanting to keep all options open, Jms finally accepted.

What do you want? he sent huffily.

Temporary team-up. Until we get out of this.

I'm listening.

We take down Jkb and present thugs together, then go separate ways. If more of Lorenz's cygoons show up, we run.

How do you intend to do either?

I've got my tricks. Some offense, some defense.

Same, Jms sent, not wanting to give away his gadgets yet.

Look, how soon is your shield ready? Can you handle one or two of them?

I can't take more than a single direct close range shot in the next 30 seconds, but I can handle a few thugs.

I mean it about the team-up. I can't get out of this on my own. I doubt you can, either.

Alright already. I've got assassin-grade weapons on me. I can take down a few for sure. If I can get past their guns.

Yna emoji-sighed. *I can take out a few guns. Be ready.*

This exchange had gone on during the brief talk with Jkb. Yna springs forward.

With her insanely fast reflexes, she kicks two gun hands, breaking them. She then tackles Jkb, but he's unmovable and deflects her attack easily, her whole body flying away from him.

Jms is just realizing that Yna has moved when he acts, zipping in behind her and lashing out with his secret weapon: the Micro. blade.

The Micro.blade is top tier military-grade assassination gear. A six-inch, nearly invisible blade attached to a five-inch-thick handle, it's a molecular-edge cutting knife held rigid by a powerful magnet, can cut through most metals like hot wire through ice. The handle generates a very small electromagnetic field around the blade, so it also disrupts most circuitry, bio-cyber enhancement or otherwise.

Jms isn't as fast or as big as Yna, but he can move when he needs to. He weaves between enemies, blade flicking out across necks and shoulders, wrists, and even other weapons if he can't get close enough. Usually, he sneaks up on someone for a takedown, but here, he just needs to buy more time.

Jkb is just tossing Yna aside, so Jms goes for him, hoping he'll still be distracted. Jms gets up close and stabs into Jkb's shoulder.

Jkb turns his down-swinging arm into a warding blow on Jms. Jms can't get away in time, so he sets his shoes to zero friction again and braces himself. The blow hurts but merely pushes him away instead of otherwise shattering bones. Jms barely catches himself on the wall, bringing the friction back to normal. He then sprints away from another cygoon lining up a shot on him. They fire, but the Push.shield deflects it, thrusting him out of the way. He wasn't in the direct blast, so the push hadn't been full power. It's still enough to send him stumbling, though. He turns it into a roll behind two cygoons fighting Yna. She's mostly downed one, though they're stubbornly hanging on to her leg, and she's grappling with the other, trying to keep them from aiming their gun at her head. Jms shakes off the Push.shield's disorientation and gains his feet, when Yna's body blurs again. Her knee extends, breaking the one cygoon's face and sending them sprawling on the ground. Simultaneously, her forearm flexes, capturing and crushing the other cygoon's gun in one swift action. Then, she chops that cygoon in the throat, dropping them as well.

She and Jms turn to each other and take a breath to speak.

Jkb hollers, "You think you're something? You think this'll stop me?"

They turn to Jkb, who's lifting his left arm while his right hangs dead and twitching. His large plated-hand unfolds to reveal gun barrels. More things click into place, a small motor begins priming.

"Kill all my flunkies? Bust up my arm? I got more! I got way more!" he shouts. His eyes light up with targeting software.

Yna msged Jms as soon as the arm began unfolding. *Can you survive a fall at this height?*

Not a fall, but I'll catch myself.

Good. Get ready.

For wh-

Yna grabs Jms. His endocrine.boost had been pumping his veins with a special adrenal-cocktail, so everything's sped up, or rather slowed down, for him. He watches as Jkb's arm-gun comes online and begins firing, orange flowers blooming at the barrels. He sees Yna pull him into a bear hug against her, noting her firm, muscular flesh beneath him. He sees her legs squat down against the heavy desk. Then, much faster than the molasses movement of everything else, they fully extend, shooting her, and him, off the ground. They quickly approach the breached window, the skyline broadening before them, ready to devour them whole.

Then they're outside, falling away from the building quickly. Bullets zing past. Yna releases Jms with a push and a parting msg. *See ya around, Jms.* Then she's sailing off at an increasingly diverging angle. SM4K flashes warnings at him, so he brings his left hand up, readying the grpl.hk program. His modified arm shoots out a grapple through his permeable sleeve, grabs a far corner of the building, and swings him away from the window Jkb's still firing from. The program takes over, and alternating grpl.lines shoot out to ease his descent to a safer level, where he'll call for a ride.

What an end to a lunch.

The food wasn't even that good.

***

Back at his biocon, Jms stretches out on his bed, surrounded by food packages he'd ordered while waiting to hear from Hns. After an assignment goes sideways like this, Hns usually checks in, whines at him, then asks for something else almost immediately. Jms knows the routine but needs some good food to deal with it.

Hns' large, infantile face takes up the wallscreen as he hovers too close to the camera, his sparse eyebrows furrowed above sparkling baby blues. His monotone fills the room. "I don't get how you failed so easily."

"I didn't fail," Jms reiterated angrily, munching on a Cheetos Oreo. "I just didn't get one-hundred percent data from CardinalZero. Most of it wasn't valuable anyway. The only thing that's of value is that thing Carr mentioned, 'GreenFutures.'" Jms sips some A.1. Whiskey straight from the bottle and adds, "I almost died for this, y'know."

"So do better next time," Hns says absently. "Yes, either the incomplete data pull corrupted it, or it was a decoy from start. 'GreenFutures' however, is pulling up a lot on my network. Mostly rumors, future project, a lot of bigwig attention, but nothing concrete."

"So whattya want me to do?"

"Keep digging." Hns signs out, the wallscreen going to an aquarium livefeed screensaver.

Jms grumbles and drops his head onto the bed.

***

The next day, Jms organizes a quick acquisitions gig. His team's been scouring corporo-mail for more notes on GreenFutures, and something turned up on FenceExchange. They'd been doing heavy overseas trade, buying up land only to sell it within hours—hours Jms'll bet it took someone to check out said land for something. The oil cache? But in the recent twenty-four hours, with the CardinalZero raid fresh on the feed, FenceExchange has been slowing their buys down. It's a small but steady trickle. Hns suspects they know something, and Jms bets it's the case, too. But they can only do so much at a distance; FenceExchange is no slouch on their cyber defenses. This'll take an intimate approach.

Most operational info acquisition uses him as the needle piercing the shield of the security system, the remote team powering through their target's databases like the phalanx following the single spear-wielding Spartan. FenceExchange is on high alert; Jms needs the whole team present.

They hijack an airship, an automated shipping container as long as four old-timey tractor-trailers floating just above smog level. It's Jms and five others: a bunch of alt-hack kids, young folk in their twenties, sporting chains, spikes, analogue timepieces, and neon glowing filament hair in bizarre styles. The most senior is a chunky guy with a messy mushroom of black hair, leading them. A skinny, greasy guy with tangled hair over his eyes sits down cross-legged with his tab-screen and doesn't make a peep. A curvy girl with hair striped neon green and yellow is second-most talkative. An NB person with heavy eye shadow coordinates between everyone else, then another skinny girl with ratty braids with glowing tips hauls a backpack into their space. The backpack contains not more gadgets like Jms expects (they all carry their own equipment themselves) but snacks: MonsterPower drinks and GamerKibble in wearable delivery systems.

They may be in the foggy, sparsely-populated area, but Jms still wishes they'd dressed more appropriately for a heist. Wouldn't have killed them to lose the glowing shigg.

But aside from questionable fashion choices, they're all business, getting rigs set up quickly and efficiently, commandeering the airship. They steer it towards their target, a server building. With FenceExchange in alarm state, they need to be close to directly implement their acquisition programs. If they still can't get in from just outside the building, Jms will be going in to acquire hard access.

The programming team is in-sync—all rigs are networked together, and in smooth, fast nonverbal messages, they tackle different angles, handing off tasks to each other as they take down the proverbial giant virtually. They reach a plateau, then signal to Jms—by msg rather than just talking to him right there—that it's his turn. Jms nods and steps off the airship hovering at sixty-five thousand feet in thin clouds.

He extends his grapl.hk to the building, drawing himself

in and towards the desired floor. His smart.suit is in expanded impact-absorbing mode, but as soon as he lands, it transforms into sneak.mode. He then walks up the building's side on grippy, ninety-five percent friction shoes and gloves. He locates the regulation air vent.

Jms wiggles in, coughing a bit until his suit creates a balaclava for navigating the dusty, twisty vents, then plops down into the server room. He can be loud now; his team has turned all security systems and bots away from noticing him. He plugs a network tap into a server. He gets an alert from his team that a rather persistent alarm started and they're having trouble quieting it. They've kept it from reaching FenceExchange HQ, but he, Jms, must do something from inside.

Jms brings out his red left hand to reach its claw-fingers into another server port. Closing his eyes to concentrate, he guides SM4K about until they find the security systems.

/Hardware>server.073>unknown object>signal alarm/

Jms shuts this off. So much easier within the system itself.

This done, he msgs his team to let loose with the heavy programming. His retina.screen shows their successive hits to FenceExchange, a broadside of codes and sequences. He can't see them from here, but he imagines a bunch of stone-faced glowing wireheads typing away furiously into their modded rigs. By the time Jms climbs back out of the vents, replaces them, and grapples back to the airship, he finds the team exactly as he imagined. Nobody even looks up when he arrives.

It doesn't look too impressive from the outside, but Jms knows they're moving virtual mountains. While they all have their own cy-connections to networks, allowing all sorts of handsfree moves, they're so accustomed to manual programming that they can do both simultaneously. They're actually doing work equal to that of a whole programming floor from the early two-thousands. This sort of digital firepower could've taken down a major nation back then. Now, it's cutting through security measures like an industrial-grade torch to a titanium bank vault.

Things go swimmingly by Jms' progress levels, until he gets a msg from an unknown sender. They all get it simultaneously. The team's reaction is subtle, maybe a mouth muscle twitch or eyebrow quiver. The msg opens itself and autoplays a video to all of them at once. A Japanese-descent man of indeterminate age under a digital kaleidoscopic filter, a goatee and long hair his only distinguishing features, plays across their retina.screens.

"Greetings. I see you're hard at work tackling the FenceExchange security system. I do not represent them, but I do have a stake in what you're stealing. By all means, proceed. But there will be immediate consequences. If you wish to avoid negative impacts, I suggest you cease your collective actions now. Personal fallout will commence shortly."

The video finishes, replaced by a black backdrop sixty-second timer countdown.

Some team members shake their heads, smirking at the warning and how none of their online actions are being attacked or affected. The video's just a warning, if an odd one. No one has even called the local security teams or authorities.

Then, the timer changes to thirty seconds, and a face appears at center. It's a social profile unknown to Jms, some older woman with messy, curly dark hair. But she's apparently known to Mushroom-cut Hacker, because he stiffens, his mouth dropping open. The timer ticks down, everyone looking internally at their screens, unsure what to do.

The Neon-striped-hair Hacker girl says, "Isn't that your . . ."

"Shh," Mushroom-cut says, brows furrowing. Then, as the time ticks down to twenty seconds, a red target appears over the image of his loved one. The man's eyebrows shoot up. Two of the others glance at each other, exchanging unreadable looks. Mushroom-cut murmurs, then says louder, "There's no way—they couldn't . . . It's a bluff . . ." He trails off.

They all watch the timer finish, the crosshairs flashing brighter and heavier, until the image beneath darkens and vanishes. The screen says, 'Target reached.' Then the center shows another person's image, and a new timer starts at twenty-five seconds. Ratty-braids Hacker girl sits up straight, her mouth a small 'O.' She bites her lip through the same crosshairs-countdown overlay until that image fades. Afterwards, she seems to shut down, slumping over, just staring.

This continues through the whole team. Jms finally recognizes who the threat-sender is (since the digital filter kept it from being identified by SM4K) — Gbe Ikari, head of 4B. He's a known recluse, managing his vast corporate empire and profits from his high castle. No in-person contact with employees. Never leaving his fortress, for all anyone knew. He contacts people frequently through video calls, always some egoistic performance driving his steely eyes and sly, barely-mobile mouth.

Jms hadn't ever confirmed how Ikari handles business enemies. Digital, distant methods are in his purview. But would he harm someone's relatives? Jms isn't sure. He only knows he has no such weakness himself, has nothing to worry about. If Gbe wants to track down his parents and do something to them, he's welcome to. They never had time for Jms; he could give a shigg.

But the team feels otherwise. Mushroom-cut has abandoned his rig, is off to the side making a call to his mother/aunt/whoever (and hasn't gotten a response). Ratty-braid girl's just rocking back and forth, the Heavy-eye-shadow NB Hacker's looking at their retina.screen muttering in disbelief, and well, the Thin-greasy Hacker guy isn't doing anything different. He's still just typing away with the same speed and coldness as before. Neon-stripes girl is near panic, as the timer-countdown finally selects someone she knows, a young, red-haired girl.

Mushroom-cut comes back, saying, "Not getting an answer. But . . . it doesn't mean—they could've just cut comms . . ."

Latching onto that idea, Jms says, "Exactly. It's 4B's Gbe Ikari. He doesn't send thugs to your house to break knees; he just sends nasty digital threats. Ignore it and finish the job."

But Neon-stripes isn't having it. "How do you know? I can't reach her either. What if she's really in trouble? She's on post-surgery machine-assist. If the hospital programs get disrupted, it'll shut down."

Mushroom-cut approaches to offer comfort but stands awkwardly there as she tears up, hyperventilating.

Jms steps between them, staring them both down. "It's not real. Psychological warfare meant to cause panic. Put it aside and finish the job." When no one besides Grease-boy looks ready to keep working, he sighs and says, "I'll double your bonuses. All of you. Just finish it."

Mushroom-cut looks like he's considering but is the only one. Neon-stripes is wringing her hands, and Heavy-eye-shadow's biting their lip and not meeting Jms' eyes.

Then Jms is notified by SM4K of an approaching vehicle below. Not manned, auto-drive. Facing its direction, Jms tracks it and looks at the signal commanding it. He turns around.

"Hey! What the hell are you doing?" he addresses Grease-boy.

Grease-boy doesn't answer. He finishes his task and packs up his personal gear, throwing down the auto-feed system. He walks to the airship's edge.

The approaching vehicle's a mini airship for smaller air-delivery, about the size of three people lengthwise.

Jms walks up to Grease-boy. "You idiot, you just hijacked a vehicle without any track-covering, announcing to everyone that you—therefore we—are here."

Jms grabs the man's shoulder, but he just shrugs it off and hops onto the vehicle, which he virtually drives off.

Mushroom-cut rubs his scruffy face, "Oh, his sister has implant-rejection seizures. If her auto-meds aren't on schedule, she gets real bad."

"Frett all this," Jms hisses. On his retina.screen, he has SM4K grab all the programs the team started and re-initiate them. It's a lot slower with just SM4K commanding them, but they'd gotten enough of a start he can finish the job. He just needs a few more minutes implementing programs at this proximity.

The timer-window app pops back on his screen. Jms sneers. "Go ahead. Who you gonna get? My old caseworker?"

The timer starts at ten seconds. The profile image that shows is his own.

Jms laughs. He continues working.

The team's mostly immobile but take some notice, looking

at Jms fearfully. Some glance about in the quiet, foggy level of skyscraper forest, wondering what form the punishment will take. A targeting rocket? An assassin bot? An innocuous drone set on kamikaze? Or a cygoon to break Jms' neck?

As the clock ticks down, slowly, inevitably to one, nothing can be seen or heard.

Zero.

Still and quiet. Nothing.

Jms crows. "See? Toldja! Just an empty threat."

The team looks on bewildered as he finishes the job by himself, tying all the digital loose ends. The major data transferred back to MannGo HQ, so Jms will see the results from his home's secure link.

He disconnects the program interface and looks at the team's sorry remains. He scoffs. "While you may have started the job, you failed to complete, and as such will only be paid half. Y'all better be back to work by tomorrow." Then, he grapples off, leaving the team on their own.

Jms returns to his building's base to find his biocon missing. In its place is a smoking crater on the building's side. Flashing authorities and emergency lights hover around its level, far above his head. He stands there, gaping at the absent biocon. The concierge says apologetically what the authorities told him. Jms will only understand later, reading the report that he can't hear now through the rage boiling in his head. The attackers used drone-sent remote detonation devices for precise and clean demolition of his place and everything in it. Burning debris rained over the streets below without affecting any surrounding cons.

Ikari'd been good on his threat after all.

***

Jms is holed up in a HyattMarriott, letting his tools charge and his smart.suit reknit itself while picking through a variety of comfort food he's ordered from room service. The dispenser elevator's still dinging and unloading things onto the cart. Once SM4K had scrubbed the room for physical and virtual dangers, he'd sent Hns a quick update. Then, he took a long hot shower, filled with screams of rage and beating his fists on tiled walls.

While drying off, he sees several missed calls, all Hns. Jms msgs that he's in no mood to talk. Minutes later, Hns emails him, another lead to follow. Jms bitterly bites into a Cinnamon Toast Crunch drumstick and reads it.

PrincipalFirst and Residents are teaming up on some initiative out in the Midwest. Or so it appears. He sits up, interest piqued. Big funds are shifting, possibly masking other deals. Especially since Hns' network shows the businesses involved, with more lined up to buy in. An unknown keeps popping up, a logo of 'GF' shaped as a small, round, green tree. Jms can't find anything else under this logo. Searching it leads to a site with the same symbol enlarged and the words "coming soon."

Reading further into the PF & R initiative, Jms finds they're hosting a small shindig in Sal Lake City, in some new 'SunTower' ecodesign structure. This is an in-person-only meeting. Hns' corp ID got an invite, so Jms can go as his rep.

Jiggling his leg, he decides to go. He's full of angry energy after his biocon was bombed to hell, and he needs to do something.

He's just RSVP'd when he gets a private msg from a yna.hopper@amgro.com. Jms rolls his eyes, then blinks an accept command.

From: yna.hopper@amgro.com
To: jms.carver@manngo.com
Subject: Need Your Help

Oh good, just saw your RSVP to the PF & R thing. We were also invited.

Listen, I need to ask a really big favor. I'm sure you're already headed there for MannGo, but I need your help. My CEO, Mdy Flores, vanished after going to an early meeting with PF & R & just sent me an SOS. I think they're playing games hard & fast, & this meeting's a setup. But regardless, I need to go see what they did with Mdy.

Pls respond asap. I booked a flight for 2 to SLC, UT.

Yna.Hopper

Jms groans. It definitely sounds like a trap. He wants to cancel his RSVP, but he remembers how Yna helped him against Jkb Lorenz. He wouldn't have made it out alive if not for her. Jms grits his teeth. He owes her.

Living on the street, growing up with other fosterkids, you learn the weight of respect, reciprocity, and repercussions. If somebody did something for you, looked out for you, you owed them. Paying that back showed respect and also showed your own worth. Not paying it back got you repercussions.

Yna's technically competition, her and AmGro. But Yna's also a fosterkid. She knows.

Does that mean she's using him? That she knows he'll feel this way after helping him out and is now roping him into this?

Jms had been ready to go on his own. Yna's now asking him to go knowing it'll probably be a trap. He can prepare now.

Sighing, he replies, dictating, "Ok, I'm in. When's the flight?"

***

The flight's DeltaBlue, business class. Jms sips Coke Royal whiskey, not for the alcohol (alcinhib's on, trying to stay sharp) but for the taste. The sweet and smokey flavor helps him ignore Yna's nervous chatter. She won't stop talking, but not about anything he wants to know. He asks about her enhancements, stuff he's never seen even through his connections. But she deflects, then gets into other matters, like trying to revive the sustainable energy business sector. She's animated, going into detail after detail with bright-eyed innocence, like the planet can still be saved, like it's not permanently poisoned, like the corporations haven't already won and are just fighting over the scraps of a corpse before it grows cold.

Yna says something, her tone questioning. Jms accesses his iReader, seeing the highlights from her rambling.

"Right, the GloDay project," he says. "I've heard of that. Is that any different than the Station-X or whatever?"

Yna narrows her eyes at him. "Not quite. It's more sustainable overall, creating its own self-reliant ecosystem. Those other projects are more flash and pandering to the Uppers than anything." She seems about to say more but stops. Her eye movement suggests retina-screen interactions.

Jms shrugs mentally and checks his own screens, SM4K showing checklist done, all tools charged and testing fine.

Yna again opens her mouth, pauses, and says, "Are you Ok? You seem . . . really distant. Distraught. Something."

Jms lets out a breath. *Should I tell her about my biocon?*

"Look, my last mission went bad, had backlash. My place got bombed."

"O.M.G.!"

"Yeah. Gbe Ikari." It doesn't cost him anything to say this. SM4K reads her vitals—breathing, eye movement, heart rate—looking for signs of prior knowledge. But no, her surprise is genuine. He continues, "So, yeah, I'm a little edgy. Is Ikari satisfied or still after me? Does anyone else wanna swing at me?" He shifts in his seat, rolling his neck.

Yna's quiet a moment, gaze inward. "Is Ikari involved in this? Taking Mdy Flores?"

Jms shrugs and swigs the last of his Coke Royal. "No idea. Ikari's usually a shoot-from-the-distance type, doesn't use cygoons. With him, everything's digital or drones. This could be someone else entirely."

Yna sighs. "Guess we'll see. At least we're ready for them."

Jms hopes that's true.

The Sal Lake City area stretches out before them as they exit the jet. The great basin's unique geography and weather patterns make pollution a major issue. Besides a re-revival in Mormonism, it brought a spate of green energy industry: the production, use and maintenance of Air.scrubbers. As big as skyscrapers or as small as portable oxygen tanks, they filter pollutants and moisture out of air and then purify the H_2O. Useful since, as the climate worsens, the lake dries up further, exposing more arsenic. Airborne, it poisons the air. One doesn't walk around without an air.mask for long. The large tower Air.scrubbers are seen and heard humming throughout the city: soaring, dark, ominously buzzing machines futilely fighting the smog, struggling to make the place livable.

While waiting for a LyftCab, they adjust their in-flight provided air.masks, Jms trying to make his comfortable. Yna puts hers on halfway, ineffectively, and forgets about it. Jms wonders what she knows that he doesn't. He notices a local sitting on a bench/bus shelter. An obscenely large man, abdomen spilling over onto the bench, face ruddy under a sports hat, he squints at Jms while huffing into a portable Air.scrubber. His model also doubles as an oxygen provider, which would be helpful if his face/head wasn't too big for the mask piece. Jms looks in open disgust, then turns away.

"Yew folks from outta' town?" the man gasps around his mask.

Jms refuses to turn around and reply, but Yna glances over and nods.

"Y'here to see our Air.scrubber plants? Finest indus'ry this side of the US of A."

Yna smiles politely. "If time permits, we'll take a tour."

The man nods proudly, hacking and wheezing into his mask without breaking eye contact, then says, "We gon' clean the States up and keep jobs away from them dirty-"

"Our ride's here," Jms interrupts. He jumps in, hoping Yna'll hurry up. He gives the auto-driver the address while she enters.

"What's your problem?" she asks, pulling her mask down.

Jms removes his as well in the clean-aired interior. "I don't give a shigg about some hillbilly's pride in a useless industry in a dying city."

"Why's it useless? The Air.scrubbers are actually pretty effective."

"It's too damn late!" Jms spits. "Pollution's never going away, we're too reliant on systems that don't have effective sustainable alternatives, and the methods to reduce pollution/waste can't keep up with our consumption rates, let alone undo the damage our predecessors did. And I don't just mean air and water pollution. I mean *genetic* pollution. That jackass is sitting on three or more generations of poison-induced health issues—"

"That's not his fault!"

"Maybe, but his stupid mindset's not helping. None of this shit is." Jms gestures at the Air.scrubber factories they're passing as they head to the outskirts.

"When did you become so hopeless and bleak?" Yna mutters.

"When I was born into Fostercare, parents too busy 'saving the planet' to raise me. Good job, mom and pops. You did it; we're all saved."

Yna falls into a sullen silence that carries them the rest of the way.

Jms leans back, crosses a leg. His parents had been too busy with eco-conservation to raise him, call him, or even send him a birthday card. He learned to hate holidays and birthdays. What's the point if there's no one else to celebrate with? And it's not like he got any real gifts, just stupid state donations, general stuff, never money—another flight-risk. Everyone in foster care was hurting, and the easiest way to deal with it was to hurt others. He learned real early not just how to fight but how to not get too injured. How to outsmart an enemy rather than fight them head-on. He started stealing as a way to dissuade bullies (other fosterkids, siblings, parents, cousins, neighbors). He didn't steal for himself but to trap off other people, get the bullies in trouble when they were discovered with the stolen goods. Besides, he was a foster kid; he was expected to be a thief, a sneak, a liar, a hood. Might as well be good at it.

So he survived. Got minimum ed. levels for his own use, especially with technology, then became a better thief and con. Even if his file had a red flag a mile long from being a foster child, if you're good enough, they can't actually pin anything on you; they can only assume. *Assume all you want. Bastards got nothing on me.*

Jms sneers, staring off into the distant wasteland.

The SunTower is aptly named: a lone-standing skyscraper one-hundred-twenty floors tall, made of flashy, smooth ecodesign. There are intervals between adjustable solar panels for conference room windows.

As Jms and Yna enter the structure, the revolving sealed-glass doors envelope them like a bubble, bringing them into a comfortably cool, humming lobby. A smiling attendant greets them and leads them into a waiting elevator. She presses her hand to a pad. It reads her 'prints and turns green, and the elevator ascends.

At level thirty, the elevator becomes transparent. Now Jms sees into every floor. They pass a gamer den with people laying down, standing, or sitting in complicated gyroscopic rigs, playing a variety of games through screens or goggles. There's a download/ deep dive den with people in various states of repose, their cy-implants connected (wired or wireless) to entertainment servers. They pass a rave scene, people in everything from tight and revealing nightclub wear to business suits dancing to thumping beats and pulsing lights. They even see a fancy 1920s night club scene, a full brass band playing bouncy music.

After a many more floors, they finally come to the general conference floors. Nicely furnished and carpeted rooms and halls hold tables and chairs, glasses and refreshments, all pleasing to the eye. There are several of these. A few are even in use, suited corporate folk smiling while getting non-alc drinks and hors d'oeuvres. Finally, the elevator stops at the 89th floor. This floor's not see-through. Jms and Yna exchange glances.

The attendant simpers. "This floor is for more private functions." She presses her hand to a pad which, reading her 'prints, turns green. The door opens.

The floor resembles most corporate office spaces, smooth but sharp-edged in dark colours. The attendant leads them around twisting hallways past empty glass-walled meeting rooms until the hall ends. Large, opaque doors open onto a large meeting room. A long table and empty chairs stretch into darkness. Only the nearest end is lit and visible. The other end is in total darkness. Jsm strains to hear anything, has SM4K search through his senses for any sort of vibrations that could tell him anything. Nothing. Must be sound dampening.

He sends a msg to Yna to see if she can pick up anything but only gets an error. They're jamming personal comms? He tries his team as well; same error. He glances over at Yna, trying to convey his worry and warning at once. She looks at him and seems to pick it up.

The attendant says, "Sorry if you're experiencing communications loss. We at SunTower offer the best in security and privacy for the comfort of our partners in handling . . . *delicate* information." She beams more brightly than ever. Then, she leaves.

Jms turns to Yna, scoffing. "So what, we're just supposed to talk to each other now?" He means it as a joke, but Yna's unnerved. She's quiet, shoulders tense, and her eyes keep shifting to the dark end. Jms' ignores it. Of course the trap's over there, and/or the trap orchestrators. He's not giving them the pleasure of showing fear or worry. They'll come at him when they do.

Yna then turns to him, eyes shining, focused, staring hard at him. She starts talking. "My, what intrigue, hmm?" Each sentence has long pauses in between. "What deal do you think they'll offer? ... Think we'll figure out more about *that* project?"

Jms quirks an eyebrow. *What's her deal?*

Then, SM4K updates him about the room. SM4K may not have 'Fi right now, but it's a powerful helper program on its own, using his own neuralnet, which is a beast. It calculates the length of the room, including the areas the screen and dampening field are hiding. The orchestrators could be as far as twenty or as close as twelve ft away.

Jms sees Yna's ear twitch, her brow furrowing in concentration. She might be doing her own investigating.

The darkness lifts, and the room's other end is revealed. Jms still can't access his network, so the 'privacy' dampener's still up.

At the long meeting table's end are a sharply dressed woman and man in matching suits, tans, smiles, and haircuts. Standing a bit behind them is a group talking quietly with their backs to Jms—SM4K tries to identify them through his personal memory stores, but it's hard without visible faces.

The two not-twin twins unfold their hands and speak in unison. "Hi, we're Szy Beals and Csy Barden, co-founders of Residents. We hope you're enjoying SunTower."

Ugh, Jms thinks, *they're simultalkers. Gross.* Yna's lip curls as well. Simultalkers are people who've synced their thoughts in a small hivemind. Some do it for better romantic partnership, others for business and planning. Jms wonders if these two did it for both reasons.

A black man in a silver pinstripe suit peels off from the group and joins the other two. He's muscular but flashy, bearing silver rings on his fingers, diamond studs in his ears, and a silver cam pin on his tie. His haircut, Jms notices, is razor-cut—done on the streets by someone good.

"And this is Rgy Lewis of PrincipalFirst," the duo says. "We formed a partnership in these . . . interesting times to forge a better path ahead into the uncertain future. To make it more certain." Szy and Csy share a look.

Jms shivers. *So creepy, like a fretting mirror.*

"So, what's the deal you're offering?" asks Yna, still eyeing the unidentified group in the back.

"PrincipalFirst and Residents have joined up with . . . another starting venture with enormous potential. The deal we want to offer you is . . ."

They slide away from each other as the group behind them parts like a curtain. Behind them all, at the far end of the room on a leatherine couch, is Mdy Flores, AmGro's head, disheveled but alive. Yna's boss and friend—or more, judging from Yna's changed look and breathing. Mdy sits in a frumpled suitdress, staring down at the ground in exhaustion.

Csy and Szy turn back, looking at Yna, speak in unison. "Give us all holdings and control of AmGro, and we'll release Mrs. Flores into your care." They have identically-molded grins.

Jms looks to Yna. Her eyes are large and watery, her face a twitching mask.

Then, the mask falls away, and she spits, "Shigg on that! Shows how much you know; she wouldn't want that. And there's no guarantee you'll leave us alive. Nice thought-out plan!"

Mdy actually responds to this. She looks up, life in her eyes, smiles tiredly, and nods.

Jms scoffs. "And me? My boss ain't here. What's your threat to me?"

The not-twins mechanically grin brighter. "Hand over everything from your company, and we'll let you all walk out alive."

Jms looks at Yna.

They burst out laughing.

Szy and Csy's amusement dims as they look at each other confusedly.

PrincipalFirst's Rgy looks annoyed, fiddling with his lapels.

Jms says, "My boss ain't dumb enough to give me that kind of power, but even if he were, I still wouldn't."

Csy and Szy raise left eyebrows. "Why?"

Jms sneers. "Just to spite you."

Rgy nods, shrugging slightly; he understands. Perhaps he had grown up on the same streets as Jms.

Szy and Csy sigh, folding their hands. "Then I guess this meeting is over." The group behind them leave.

Jms and Yna look at each other, perplexed. "You're letting us go?" Jms queries, eyeing the door behind him.

Szy and Csy simply open their hands, smiling dumbly.

Yna lets out a breath and mutters, "Watch my back," then heads to Mdy. Mdy stands with difficulty and lets Yna support her as they walk back to their exit. Jms watches the creepy not-twins the whole time. They even blink together.

Mdy squints blearily and mumbles, "Drugged."

Jms nods. *This'll slow us down.*

The door opens, and two cygoons enter, aiming guns at them. They're enhanced to be fast, but they're not at Jms' level. He dives for them faster, slapping their firing guns away and feeling the heat on his hands. He shoves one behind him to Yna, fighting the other slowly—or so it seems in his adrenal rush. He manages to wrestle away control of the cygoon's gun, using it to shoot him in the head. He pushes through to the next group he sees coming in, fires on their gun arms, then fires twice more into their chests. He feels a bullet hit his push.shield in the side, sending him bouncing back a bit.

Yna's pulling Mdy into the hall behind Jms, when around the corner comes a man in a shiny trenchcoat with a subsonic autogun. Yna pushes Jms and Mdy down while she leaps up, blurring to the ceiling and landing at an angle on Trenchcoat's chest. A few low burping noises sound as shots escape the autogun, sinking harmlessly into the walls. She kicks his throat in and grabs the gun strap. Then, she helps Mdy up. Jms struggles up himself, nostrils flaring. He motions for the subsonic-autogun. Yna hesitates, her eyes dilating. He motions again, and she gives it up. He swings back into the meeting room to see the two eerily-grinning Residents partners. Panting, he looses subsonic bullets, cracking the table in half diagonally and blowing apart Csy's head. Szy's hair is ruffled. When her partner-twin's death registers, she gasps, eyes wide, twitching and stuttering, "F-f-f-f-" spittle flying from her convulsing mouth. Jms nods; his work's done here.

He rejoins Yna. She has Mdy behind her, gripping her belt. Jms takes point, the sub-auto in front, another gun in his belt. The elevators are locked and best avoided anyway, so they hunt for the stairs and head down. Each landing has a clear glass wall so you can see the floor you've just reached—and reinforcements can also see you. Jms cautiously approaches each new floor, but the next few are empty.

They pass an active conference floor, and some folks stop socializing to stare open-mouthed at Jms' party. He realizes they're all blood-spattered, he's openly carrying, and Mdy looks possibly kidnapped. Jms smiles and waves, then keeps going down. Many, many floors down. They meet no resistance for ten, fifteen, twenty floors, but they don't let their guard down.

When they reach the 'party' floors, they're barely noticed. But the floor plan also changes. Suddenly, the stairs down are on the opposite side. They have to pass through part of the floor to exit.

Great.

Yna towers over most partygoers, so she pushes ahead, while a still-dazed Mdy follows. Jms watches their six. This floor's decorated in peak 1970s "Disco Fever," so everything mimicks that aesthetic, right down to the use of the "powder rooms." Jms see people leaving, wiping noses and rubbing excess powder into gums. No violence awaits them here, just people mindlessly dancing to terrible old music, sweating and grinding into each other. Yna bumps them aside, and eventually, they reach the stairs.

The next party's flavor is Antebellum Southern US ball. Gentlemen groups smoke cigars in a study and women in large basket dresses congregate on a holo-veranda while couples whirl on the ballroom floor. Yna plows right through the dancers, ignoring those she throws off or who give her nasty looks. Jms smirks while watching their back.

Next is the 1990s "Rave"-era party. Too many blacklight/

glow-in-the-dark decorations, people dancing to repetitive beats. They stumble a bit in the darkness and flashing lights. Jms can't get away fast enough.

The next level is a roaring 1920s, prohibition-style party. Alcohol and bad dancing.

"These aren't even in chronological order!" Jms complains, brushing off multiple giggling drunks. This feels too easy. No one else has come after them, and he feels weirdly forgotten. His survival instincts tell him this is when someone smart would move—when prey become complacent. He clenches his teeth tight and flexes his muscles but keeps his gun hand loose. Tightening that could—

Pop, pop, pop!

Jms swings towards the sound with his sub-auto, nearly pulling the trigger, before realizing it's several champagne bottles popping. Some revelers in old-style haircuts and suits laugh uproariously, unaware they'd nearly died.

Yna had also turned to look, wary but calmer than Jms. When she turns back ahead, three security guards in angular metallic gear are raising weapons to fire.

"Down!" she shouts.

Jms blinks, and Yna's gone, the guards hitting the floor. SM4K gives him snapshots moments later of what happened; Yna unbuckled her belt with Mdy holding it. Then, she leapt forward with inhuman speed. Faster than anything Jms could do. Yna caught two guards in the throat with her arms. As they fell, she rotated to kick out at the third gun. It knocked into the standing guard's gut, bowling them over, also. Yna jumped back while they still struggled to breathe.

Mdy stands there, blinking at the empty belt, trying to

comprehend what happened. Yna buckles it back on, says to Jms, "C'mon! Let's go before-"

VEEEEEN.

A full-auto discharges a violent stream. People topple over; glasses and bottles shatter. It happens so fast the mayhem takes moments to set in. Yna yanks Mdy down on top of the downed guards, while bystanders take most of the bullets. Jms' push.shield deflects a few hits but knocks him over, also. Bloody bodies drop, horror dawning on their faces. Jms stumbles into an opening in the crowd and fires with his subauto. He catches two guards coming down the stairs in the throat and face. They fall gurgling. Jms runs back to collect the unfired guns and returns to Yna, who is helping Mdy up.

Pandemonium grips the partygoers. One man in crimson-stained shirt, held by others, screams hoarsely, "It hurts! I can still feel it! Get coke from upstairs! Get coke!!"

Jms and Yna head downstairs.

Some goons hide around a corner in the stairwell, to surprise them. Yna turns to them and *FFFFT!* shoots something out from under her jaw. The guards are encased in a sticky coating, like a gooey, contracting web. They can no longer see or aim weapons, as their upper torsos are solidly connected. Yna kicks them over, and they continue on.

They go through more floors, dealing with pockets of metallic security. Yna gets hit a few times around her strangely armored suit, but her bleeding stops very quickly. Jms' push.shield is nearly depleted and charging, so he's taken a few hits. The smart.suit armor has mostly held up, but he's bruised all over his torso, and his left shoulder might be dislocated. And he's limping. Doesn't remember why, but left ankle hurts. Sometimes, there are bystander casualties, sometimes not. Interesting that the security detail isn't overly picky with that. Must mean the partygoers aren't important.

Or they really want Jms, Yna, and Mdy dead.

On the medieval party level, they don't notice the security guards right away because they mistake them for era armored knights in their shiny, angular metallic gear. It's only when Jkb Lorenz steps out, his suit personalized to carry his size and mass of enhancements, that they realize their mistake. Jkb's patched up from the encounter days ago—a long time ago, it seems—at the CardinalZero lunch. But his movement's slower and jankier, especially around the right arm and shoulder, where Jms stabbed him with the micro.blade. Jkb has a mini-cannon aiming on them, carrying it easily in his left arm and lurching forward with a grim look on his mostly immobile face. Jms reluctantly drops the sub-auto.

"Youse thought you'd done me in, huh?" Jkb's eyes glow with various programs. Vicious malware attacks Jms' system, to keep him on the defensive. "They called me into this party for a chance at you." He lifts his right arm in threat, but with difficulty.

"Oh yeah? Why don't ya clap for me," Jms quips. Yna gives Jms a warning look.

Jkb's face turns degrees colder. With the gun trained on Jms, he stomps up, gait hitching and uneven. SM4K warns that the push.shield's perimeter's breached. Jkb breathes oily sourness in Jms' face.

Jkb sneers and hisses, "Funny man, huh? With yer fancy tech, still looking nice and pretty. We can fix that. Fix all that. Real slow . . ."

Jms coughs and turns away. "Can we fix your breath, first? Fuck—"

Jkb winds up to hit with his right arm, his face pinched in rage. This arm's slow enough from the injuries Jms could easily dodge if the cannon wasn't keeping him there. He's especially slow for a cy-enhancement.

Yna leaps out to the side. She zips past, kicks his cannon away.

That's all Jms needs. The cygoons haven't bothered aiming at Jms, leaving it all up to their boss, so Jms whips out his waistband gun, switching it over to the surprise he'd kept in case of bozos like Jkb. The fact that he'll get to use it on Jkb makes it all the sweeter.

Jkb's just shifting his body awkwardly to bring himself back in control and get ready to strike again. In the stretched-out seconds of Jms' adrenaline-fueled hyperfocus (which is quickly depleting, his system warns), he brings up his gun and is just able to fire into Jkb's torso before his mallet-fist careens into Jms.

Jms' push.shield activates, not at full power, but enough to halve the blow. Jms is thrown back, entire body vibrating, and he tumbles into the fall to spread out the damage. His back hurts, and his ribs and lungs ache. He struggles to breathe, let alone move.

The bullet hits and sticks in Jkb's lower left abdomen, stopped by his body-armor. He looks down and cackles. "That's it?"

Yna, held by two cygoons-in-shining-armor, looks at Jms despairingly.

Jms can barely breathe but manages a smile.

The stopped bullet explodes *Bang!* Jkb's body vibrates. His eyes widen, face frozen.

The pierce.bullet's designed for heavily armored enemies or machines. The outer shell's explosive enough to pierce armor.

This releases a smaller but durable diamond-tipped drilling bullet, which will dig and bounce around inside, just a bit slower than the average bullet.

Jkb grabs onto his body uselessly, vibrating and grunting. His eyes flash with warning notifications before they roll up into his head. His mouth opens wider, and blood froths out.

Yna's immobilized by two heavily-armored security detail, or so they think. Yna moves so their hands are right in her elbow crooks. She shifts something in her arms, then flexes her elbows like crab claws snapping shut, *CRACK*. The detail's silvery hands snap nearly in half. They scream. She elbows them both in their faces, cutting off their shouts as they drop.

Other security start to move, but Jms grabs the sub-auto and aims it at them, while Yna helps Mdy up. The crowd parts, and they head down the stairs again, Jms keeping an eye on everyone. The guards stand glaring after them or watching their boss die horribly.

They meet no more mentionable issues, until they can access an elevator again. Jms plugs into it with both his tiny red arms, cutting through all the firewalls and privacy locks. Jms sends for an armored car to pick them up when they reach ground floor.

Mdy's still dazed. As the elevator descends, Jms says to Yna, "What kind of cy-enhancements are those? I've never seen anything like that. The speed, those gadgets, all of it!"

Mdy mumbles, "'S not cy, it's biomimetics..."

Yna shushes her. To Jms, she says, "The only cy-enhancement I have is my implant and modem." She says nothing more. Jms shrugs.

Once in the armored car and heading to the airport, they relax a bit. Yna pulls out some injection ampoules and shoots them into

Mdy's neck. She perks up shortly, rubbing her head. "Ugh, like thinking through smog."

Yna asks, her hard eyes softening, "What happened?"

Mdy drinks some water and says, "They invited me to a private meeting for info on that deal—but only me. Needed my temp private line code for entry, they used that code for the SOS msg to you, but y'know, it was just a trap."

Yna nods. Jms says, "But did they take any of your data? Interrogate you at all?"

Mdy shakes her head. "No. That's the weirdest thing. They drugged me but kept me in a waiting room for who knows how long."

Yna's brows furrow. "Did you catch anything at all? Any of their other plans, maybe?"

Mdy looks thoughtful. "They were compiling some big list. Something for ... 'Green Futures,' that thing you found out about."

"Hmm," Yna nods, then quietly stares out the window.

***

At the airport, after a thorough check by Jms and his team, they determine JetAir's safe enough for the next few hours. They book a direct flight out of SLC at 2:13 AM, in five hours. They get airport hotel rooms until then, a room for Mdy and Yna and one for Jms.

Jms goes through the ritual room-debugging, creating a secure data space, then contacts MannGo. He gives his team more details now as he manages and charges his tools. Hns' auto-reply: "Busy debriefing from unconscious meditations and astral projection." Whatever that means.

Jms has again ordered room service, but their menu's slim pickings. Doritos BBQ chicken wings and Hershey's Malt liquor. They're passable. He's starving, but nervous about turning the alcinhib off. Jms' guess is PF & R has jurisdiction in SunTower, but does their reach extend to the airport hotel? He's not sure. SM4K has spy-drones and three different security programs watching the hotel building, halls, and surrounding area.

He knows when Yna approaches his door but is still surprised.

Yna knocks, then walks right in when he opens it. She's slugging back Livesaver's Jell-O shots from the hotel minibar. Her suitdress is half-off, sports undergarments showing above a rumpled skirt, her hair mussed.

"I see you're also unwinding a bit after that fricass." She motions to his meal leftovers.

Jms tips the bottle towards her. "Feel free to partake."

She shakes her head. "Hershey's doesn't mix with Jell-O shots."

"Some disagree—"

"Listen, can I ask you something?" she interrupts, turning around, hands on her hips.

"Um, OK—"

"What's your problem with me? Back in Fostercare? And now?"

Jms is taken back. "What? I never had an issue with you."

"Bullshit. You did, too."

"Look, I thought you hated me, OK?"

Yna's aghast. "Thought *I* hated you? Why?"

Jms begins pacing. "You were always mocking me with that smile. I'd do something, you'd do it better and twice as easy, then just *sneer* at me, like, 'Look how easy it is for me . . .'"

"*Sneer?!* That's what you thought? I sneered at you?" Yna shrieks, chucking the empty shot bottle at the wall.

"Well, what else was it?" Jms is shouting now, too. "You were always one-upping me, always outdoing me—"

Yna steps in front of him, her face inches from his. "I was *smiling*," growls Yna, "because I liked you!" She stands there breathing heavily.

Jms' anger evaporates. "What?"

Yna stretches her shoulders in a way Jms now finds attractive, walking towards him, forcing him to retreat to the wall. She breathes, "I liked you, wanted to be friends. I was always trying to impress you; that's why I did that, copying you, trying to get your attention, looking at you, *smiling* at you. I was a big, dumb, grinning idiot for you. And you shunned me."

Jms' back hits the wall. Yna keeps approaching, pushes her chest into his. He feels how toned she is, all muscles. Her beauty is unavoidable, and this close up, he can't ignore it anymore. Have her eyes always been this shade of violet?

"I know I left Fostercare first, but I always wondered about you. If we'd ever meet again. If we could ever finally be . . . friends." She whispers the last bit, her moist lips inches from his.

"I thought you were with Mdy?" he mutters, his hot breath bouncing off her face.

"No." She leans in and bites his lower lip.

He kisses her (a real kiss—no robo-lips!), and they melt together. Her soft, wet tongue explores every corner of his mouth as he sucks greedily at her lips. Their hands find each other's bodies, though he's slow at first. It's been a while since he's had to think about anyone's pleasure but his own, so he's uncertain what she'll like. The robot anticipated his needs and had none of its own. Then, Yna pushes his hands encouragingly to her curves and under her skirt.

Soon, they're tearing clothes off blindly. His ankle is tender, as is his ribcage. His whole torso. Most of his body. But the soreness and pain blend right into the pleasure.

As they climb on top of each other, switch positions, sweat and grab and claw at each other, grunt and breathe heavily into ears and necks, Jms can't get over the sensation of skin on skin. For all its vibrating, lubricating, skin-textured mechanisms and detailed adapting algorithms, the Purple-Siemens Skinmaster 5X doesn't compare to the real thing. It'd been a while since Jms had gotten any, but those connections had been tenuous, shallow, temporary. The numerous sex toys he's tried over the years were great sensation-wise, but always that hollow feeling after. Jms knows he probably has issues forming relationships. Grow up in a setting with no good parental role models, watching your back constantly, and see how well you relate to others. But would that affect sex, too?

As Yna's hips grind into his, he licks sweat off her chest, greedy for every drop. He grips her hips, but she puts her hands over his, growling in his ear, "Harder," until he's clawing at her waist and back, her moans thundering in his hair. He's carried away on waves, getting rockier and bigger as they climax together furiously.

Sex. Love-making. Fucking. It's all this and more. Why didn't anyone tell him it could be like this? Why's he spent all at once but famished for more? Already craving another round.

They pause to catch their breaths, staring at each other in utter disbelief.

Then they go again.

So three hours pass. When they're finally too spent, Yna heads to the shower, still casting looks back at Jms that echo his own amazement and hunger. Jms can feel himself drifting off, tangled in sheets, but knowing they've less than an hour before the flight, he needs to shower, too. With great effort, he rises out of bed and drifts into the steam, joining a glistening, wet Yna. She helps lather him up, and he does the same for her. Things start getting heavy again. But when he moans in her ear, "Yna . . .", the tone shifts. Her urgency fades into tenderness. They just end up holding each other under the water, long after they're clean.

Jms didn't realize how much he needed this, too.

There's a lot, apparently, he hadn't learned on the streets.

As the departure nears, they return to business mode. Partners on technically competing ends but temporarily working together. They dress, double-check their equipment, and suit up. Yna checks if Mdy's getting ready, then she comes back briefly to crush herself against Jms. She kisses hard like she's trying to press herself into him, to devour him or be devoured.

Finally, Mdy knocks on the door. They straighten up and put on game faces, like they have to go back to being adults and acquaintances again.

Mdy's eyes flick briefly between them. She says, "Got an aircab with my corporate ID."

Jms says, "Why?"

"So enemies have a decoy to follow," Mdy says. "Ordered another anonymously. We'll be riding with express cargo deliveries, but it's safer."

Jms sighs. "OK, that's better."

Mdy grabs her bags and heads outside. Yna turns to Jms, eyes and face softening again. "We'll be OK." She squeezes his hand, then follows.

On the cargo plane, Jms stares out the window. He's unsure what Yna meant by 'we.' Are they an item now? Working at competing companies will be problematic. But just because they slept together doesn't mean they're married. He wants to clarify things but is unsure what exactly he wants. He's split. Knowing now that she's liked him all along and had been trying to get his attention puts everything in a different light. Complicates everything. If he and Yna get involved, she'll be a target for people like Ikari, a weakness, something that can be exploited. His chest is hot and bubbly with different feelings he's never experienced before. He wants to know her, find out how her life has been since Fostercare, what her interests are, what she wants. But at the same time, he's scared, wants to close himself off, forget this ever happened. Just go back to living his life and competing with everyone else. But he can't forget how it felt being tangled up naked with Yna, a part of her. It's confusing.

***

He wakes up forty mins from landing to an urgent call. It's Hns. The call's above emergency urgent, so he literally can't turn it off. Jms hates when Hns does that. He tries sending a msg, but the call's taking priority on his internal screen. He sighs, unhooks his restraints, and walks away down the short aisle towards the cargo section to accept the call.

"Look, this isn't secure—"

"Don't care. Found what GreenFutures is. We're going there."

"What?"

"Head here immediately—"

"I am!"

"—then we'll debrief." Hns ends the call.

Jms groans and returns to his seat. Yna looks at him inquisitively.

"Boss. Checking in."

Yna nods and turns to him. "Do you care that this is all over some dumb oil cache?"

"What?" Jms said, alarmed. He's never told her this. How could she know?

"I haven't hacked you. All my enhancements are bio. Haven't you realized that? Anyway, we got the same info." Yna nods at Mdy seated before them. "Why do you think we keep running into each other? This GreenFutures has been giving us the same breadcrumbs all along. We've heard the same rumors, same research. All pointing to the last big oil cache. Doesn't that bother you? Just more greed and pollution?"

"Sustainable methods have never been sustainable. We started too late, not enough people on board, I dunno. Not my problem."

Yna looks incredulous. "Not your problem? The environment? The planet we live on?"

"Yeah. Our ancestors screwed things up beyond repair. Everything is just a bandaid on a gaping wound. I'm just here to get paid."

"You really don't care at all," Yna states, not asking.

"All the good intentions in the world won't change things. Those Green movements a century ago didn't make a big enough shift, didn't undo enough damage, and everything since then has just been sandbags before a flood. It's not stopping nothing. We're not gonna live forever. Just enjoy the time we have now, I say." Jms shrugs.

Yna shakes her head in disbelief. Her face closes up, and she stares out her window.

Geez, thinks Jms, *she's so hung up on this*. Why does it matter what he thinks? He can feel her drifting further away, like the inevitable flood he'd mentioned, the deluge that'll wipe away humanity. He's not religious or fatalist; he's a realist. It's too fucking late. Fixing the world isn't possible and isn't his problem.

Maybe even this, Jms thought, *Yna and me, isn't meant to be*. He shrugs mentally and leans back, staring out the window across the aisle. The reassuring envelope of cold distance wraps around him. *Whatever*, Jms thinks, *don't need anybody else. Just end up getting abandoned. That's just how it is.*

***

Jms arrives back in MannGo HQ. Hns meets him in a lower conference room. Another entire-floor room with transparent wall-screen windows, another rich waste of space.

Hns wears a workout jumpsuit, though the most he does is Tai Chi yoga or whatever, and he holds a glass of putrid green stuff. He launches right into it, pulling up images and articles on a wallscreen. "So, they released more info while you were gone—"

"On a mission for you. Almost got killed again," Jms says through clenched teeth. Maybe it's jetlag, or maybe he's sick of almost dying for this pompous ass.

"—on what GreenFutures is, what they do. There's a public statement, but it's just general nonsense about sustainable energies. But what they sent me personally—are you ready for this? It'll blow your mind." Hns is excited, but he still only has eyes for the wallscreens. He hasn't looked at Jms once, yet.

"Do you realize I lost my home? It was blown up by that bastard Ikari of 4B." Jms isn't yelling, but his voice is raised trying to reach this rich maniac.

Hns finally turns to look at Jms, incredulous. "Is that what you're worried about now? This is bigger than all of us, and you're worried about a biocon?"

"It was my home," Jms hisses.

Hns shrugs. "We'll get you a new one," he says, like the issue's over. He brings up the GreenFutures site.

Jms can barely concentrate. He doesn't know what he wants, what his issue is. Maybe some acknowledgement as an actual person rather than just another tool for Hns to use? Jms isn't sure. *Can't be about the Yna thing. It was a fling, no big deal.* He bounces his knee.

Jms finally tunes in when Hns starts playing a personal vid-msg. It shows a cartoonish earth, grey and soiled. Then a tree-like design sprouts up, morphing into the GreenFutures logo. This fades into a backdrop, as a man appears at its center. He's a young-looking, light-skinned black man with impeccable hair. Jms wonders briefly where he got his haircut. Bright green eyes stare through them. His voice is clear and eloquent.

"Hi, I'm Mat Carver, CEO and head of GreenFutures. We've developed a cutting-edge process to make more sustainable energy production possible." He pauses as scientists in labcoats, their names and credentials popping up in side windows, are shown working in labs with test tubes and beakers. Testing, presumably, petroleum oil.

Mat continues. "We've discovered a procedure to recreate the conditions that create fossil fuels, petroleum oil in particular, using accelerated natural means."

Hns, grinning like a child, pointedly looks at Jms. Jms doesn't hide his eye roll.

Mat Carver: "As spokesman and head of our company, I am inviting you to a new partnership with limited spots. Join me, and let's create a new, greener future." Mat opens his arms wide as the GreenFutures logo solidifies again, shiny and rippling.

"What's so green about creating more oil?" Jms asks, more skeptical of the concept than concerned about the environment.

But Hns, laughing gleefully, either doesn't hear Jms or ignores him. He motions, and more windows come up. "The details for the invite are here. Show up at this location with lots of organic material. I've got that handled. My bamboo forest for my personal oxygen purifying is being harvested as we speak. They'll have it ready for transport within the hour. Get a team and be ready to leave, as well."

Not knowing what else to do, no home to go to, Jms takes over a floor in MannGo HQ. If Hns wants him gone, he can buy him a new biocon. He washes up in an employee shower room, applies proper med-aids to himself, and naps on a couch until Hns rings him. Hns sends a page of calculated bonuses, financial projections with this partnership and new oil production. It doesn't say what Jms' bonus will be, but he can expect a lot. There's also a page of new expensive biocons—better than his old one.

Jms sighs and gets up slowly, feeling his creaky ribs and smarting ankle.

He follows a ping to Hns' personal garage, three levels filled with different vehicles, from classic gas-guzzlers to retro solar and electric vehicles to the latest modern vehicles and aircars. Hns and the selected team wait outside an airshuttle, employees loading potted bamboo shoots so tall they have to bend a little to fit in the cargo back. They're very alive—crisp, green, and fresh smelling.

Hns' explains to no one in particular, "These are the Chinese moso bamboo, fastest growing bamboo—in fact plant—in the world. They help purify air, they can be made into eco-friendly wood planks, and they're much more sustainable than other woods, hardier even . . ."

Jms walks away to the cockpit. He sits behind the pilot. After a few minutes the team, following Hns, enters. Jms puts in earbuds to block out Hns' incessant elucidation. Hns only stops to sip his green gunk at intervals.

At one point, Jms uses the restroom and hears Hns still listing all the ways that this bamboo is an efficient plant. Jms laughs himself to and from the bathroom.

Several hours later, they arrive at a private airfield somewhere in Western Pennsylvania. A large truck's ready for their bamboo plants, and they pile into a personalized van.

Jms says to Hns, "Aren't you worried this is a trap? They could be isolating us to take us out, far away from support."

Hns scoffs. "Think I didn't plan for this?" He points outside to some specks in the distance on all sides. "Personal security drones keeping track of us. And a hired security team stationed ahead that will be following us at a distance. They'll surround the location minutes after we arrive, ready to swoop in. We'll be fine."

Jms lays back in his seat. He tries to rest, but Yna's face keeps popping into his head. Her different expressions. The taste of her breath, the warmth of her up against him. Jms brings up a mini-game to distract him, but he can't focus.

A few mins' drive takes them into mountainous areas. They take a long, winding road down to an old mining spot in a deep, manmade valley. At the dusty track's end is a large warehouse. Very large—two stadiums big and long. It looks very hi-tech for a warehouse. Jms has SM4K do a search on this style of warehouse. His service reaches here, but it's not giving him anything. SM4K detects lead layers in the walls. He whispers this to Hns.

Hns just grins and says, "It must have to do with the process. Fascinating! I hope I can see the science behind it. Just to know..." He's like a kid on Hallmarkoween. No worries at all.

This worries Jms.

They're directed by GreenFutures staff, ordinary-looking people in company coveralls, to bring their plants to the loading section. There are no mechanical means to carry them, so they have to do it all by hand.

Hns starts micromanaging everything. They take two trips to bring them inside the loading dock's outer door. Only then are they provided wheeled carts for the bamboo. The outer door shuts and locks. The inner door opens. They follow a short maintenance hallway into another anti-room with the same procedure—outer door shut, inner door opens. Jms' worried about all the security measures, though he knows it makes sense. Hns just gets more and more excited.

This last inner door opens to a large, bright storage section: the main warehouse room, judging by how long it is. It's filled with rows on rows of shelves, using bracket systems to have multiple levels of shelves. They're all filled with or being filled with plants.

Many different plants. Big, industrial forklifts carry algae vats to especially large shelves, directed by none other than Gbe Ikari, owner of 4B.

Jms is shocked not only to see Gbe Ikari here, but also in person at all. He's only ever seen digi-profiles or vids of Ikari, like the one that threatened him and his team. Ikari bears long, dark, greasy hair and a beard, and his overweight body seems unable to carry itself. A GreenFutures employee pushes him in a non-electric wheelchair. Ikari's already sickly pale, but he turns whiter still when he sees Hns and Jms. He shrivels in on himself, helpless outside his fortress and without defense drones. He's wheeled next to his vats as they're forklifted onto industrial shelves, where he's left gawking at Jms and Hns.

Hns is busy ordering the bamboo to be taken to its designated shelf.

"Hns. Hns," Jms calls.

He sees more CEOs and reps from other companies, competitors big time and smaller. InteGen, UnitedTechBusiness (UTB), CardinalZero, AmWorkersFedCreditUnion, MacroHard, CollectedWellness, Pear, FenceExchange, Civi. PrincipalFirst and Residents is just Szy Beals assisted by Rgy Lewis of PrincipalFirst, since Jms killed Csy. Szy's not operating at full capacity since her digi-twin died, and Rgy's doing the heavy lifting. Rgy see Jms and looks concerned. UTB's headed by Gta Pritam (Jkb was their go-to person, acquisitions expert like Jms), a small older Indian woman in colorful sari. She too looks shocked to see Jms.

Jms feels disquiet surrounded by so many competitors and enemies.

He walks to Hns and shakes his shoulder. "Hns!"

Hns jerks around. He does not like being touched, and is not used to anyone grabbing him. Before he can protest, Jms points out the competition surrounding them. "You see this? What're they doing here?"

And this is just one end of the warehouse. The rest is also filling with people and plants.

Hns is finally shocked into awareness. "What're they doing here?"

Jms growls, "That's what I-"

The lights blare brighter. Jms' contact lenses try to darken, but they can't handle it, at least not quickly enough. Jms is forced to shut and cover his eyes. A strange hum vibrates through the walls and ground, sending a deep thrum throughout the entire warehouse. Hns says something, but Jms can't hear. He shouts to Hns, but he's also drowned out.

VRRRRMMM

There's a large shaking jolt, as if the warehouse dropped several feet.

Disoriented and shaken, Jms picks himself, blinking blindly. He hears Hns and the team muttering to themselves. Some folks vomit on the ground.

The warehouse is gone. The shelves, plants, and people are all still there, but the warehouse around them has vanished. Only, they're not in a PA mining valley anymore.

They're in a canyon the same dimensions as the warehouse, but the steep walls are unclimbable. There's no way Jms can see out of the gulch. And the sun above beats on them with a blazing hotness strange to him. He's immediately thirsty. He shades his eyes to see everyone else looking confused. Hns is busy yelling into his watchcomm, getting no response. The drones and security team must all be gone or unreachable. Above the bewildered chatter, an electronic screech from a speaker system sounds. Jms turns in that direction of the nearer canyon end, about one-hundred feet from him. A man stands above.

It's Mat Carver of GreenFutures.

He speaks. "Your confusion is normal. You're no longer in Pennsylvania. Or your own time period. You are currently in 65 million BCE, located on what will eventually become the Seychelles island Mahé, once the tectonic plates shift a bit."

Hns is doing something on his phone with his AI system, which is probably ten times stronger than SM4K. "He's right!" Hns exclaims cheerfully. "Based on the solar radiation, we are in fact 65 million years before our own time!" He laughs and claps.

Jms wants to slug him. Doesn't he see how fucked they are?

Hns shouts up to Mat, "How'd you do this?"

Mat just shakes his head. "You should be asking *why*. And the answer is quite simple . . ."

Yna Hopper walks into view to stand besides Mat. Jms' jaw drops. Is he seeing correctly?

Mat gestures to Yna, "My partner will explain."

Yna speaks, her unmistakable voice amplified. "Organic material trapped under rock and treated to millions of years of intense pressure and heat becomes petroleum." She looks straight through Jms. "Organic. Matter." She pauses to let that sink in, then says, "This is how we plan for the future. And without you, we might actually have a chance." Her smirk is the sharpest it's ever been.

Another rumbling sounds as industrial-sized excavation beds, piled high with rocks, tilt into view. They surround the canyon.

"The answer," Mat Carver says, "is that now, you will become the oil."

The excavation beds simultaneously tip their loads, and the canyon's flooded with noise and dust.

Jms laughs as the irony hits him like a ton of rocks.

URSULA THE POWERFUL

Cheyenne Shaffer

It's time. It's time. It's time.

The incubator in the back corner of Miss Halloran's fifth grade classroom whirred, a mechanical sound that rose and fell in waves. When Patty listened for too long, it sounded like speech. Last week, she'd heard it saying *Hello* over and over. Now, it sounded more like *It's time.*

Most of the class probably couldn't even hear it. It was one-thirty, meaning science hour. The lights were off, and a nature documentary was playing. The TV must have drowned out the whirring for everyone who wasn't right next to it.

On screen, a cheetah stalked a pack of wildebeest. "She's sizing them up," the narrator said. "She'll want to target the weakest of the pack when she strikes."

"Patty," Anna Collins coughed from halfway up the room.

"What was that?" Miss Halloran asked, raising her eyes from

the papers she was grading by the window's gray light.

"Just clearing my throat."

Anna waited for Miss Halloran's attention to drop back to her desk before she turned, grinning at the girls beside her. Patty kept sketching in the margins of her notebook as if she hadn't noticed.

The classroom door clicked open, and Olivia Harrington entered, returning from the bathroom with hall pass in hand. She crept along the edge of the room, passing her row of desks without stopping. Patty sat up straighter. Olivia must be coming back to peek into the incubator.

Round and glowing from the lightbulb inside, the incubator looked like a flying saucer. It lit Olivia's face in gold as she leaned over to check on the chicks.

"Another one's coming!" Olivia announced, and every head in the room spun toward her.

Miss Halloran paused the documentary and turned on the lights as the girls flooded to the incubator. Why watch nature on TV when nature was happening right beside you?

Despite sitting so close, Patty hung back, letting the others crowd around first. They were all so alike, small girls with perfect ponytails and gossip always on their tongues. Big and awkward, Patty would never be one of them, and they never let her forget it.

Except for Olivia. She'd started at Seaside Preparatory School for Girls only weeks ago, but so far, she hadn't said one mean thing to Patty. It was a miracle. Patty wanted to make friends with her—she wanted a friend in general—but friendship was complicated. Spending time with Olivia might make her notice everything wrong with Patty. Maybe she'd only been nice so far because she wasn't paying attention. It also didn't help that Olivia made Patty feel strange. Just the sound of her name sent Patty's stomach churning.

Once everyone else seemed settled, Patty edged in as best she could for a view inside the incubator. A handful of small, white eggs lay in a circle amidst the few chicks who'd already hatched. One egg rocked back and forth, a small beak emerging occasionally to widen a hole in the shell. Minutes later, the chick broke free. Its wet down was sooty black, matching its dark feet and eyes.

"All right, class, let's find this little one a name," Miss Halloran said, reaching for the Solo cup resting by the incubator.

Inside were slips of paper bearing possible names suggested by students. Miss Halloran made them each sign their paper, as well, in case anyone suggested anything inappropriate.

"Ursula," she read from a slip. "Patty chose this one."

Patty's joy at naming a living thing withered immediately under the other girls' glares.

"All right," Miss Halloran continued, oblivious, "let's start recess a couple minutes early today."

Some girls cheered, and the room dissolved in a flurry of chatter. Interest in the new chick dwindled now that it was associated with Patty, and the crowd split into their usual groups for games and gossip.

Patty stepped into the empty space left around the incubator to study Ursula up close. A tiny fringe of feathers ran down the sides of her legs, still flattened against her feet from the wetness of her hatching, and a small crest of down piled up on her head.

"Hi," Patty cooed.

Ursula angled one beady black eye directly at Patty.

"Welcome to the world. Will you be my friend?"

Yes. The word flashed through her mind, seemingly unbidden. She frowned. Had she just answered herself, or . . .

Ursula's new legs gave out, and she flopped over. Totally normal newborn chick behavior. Patty shook her head. Had she seriously thought a chicken was communicating with her?

A group of girls shoved past, catching her attention. They huddled around the fish tank that sat on the opposite end of the counter.

"Ursula's a dumb name," Anna said.

"*The Little Mermaid*?" Ronnie Cho scoffed. "I haven't watched that since I was like seven."

"She's not even the main character," Emily Benson said. "Who names something after the bad guy?"

"Someone who looks like the bad guy?" Anna suggested, and they giggled.

Patty's chest ached. The cartoon character did look like her; Patty weighed nearly twice as much as her average classmate, after all. That was why she liked the character. Despite how Ursula looked, she was confident. In control. Powerful. She'd make a much better main character than Ariel. Who would give up something as cool as being a mermaid just to spend time with a boy, anyway? Boys were dumb.

"I think the name works."

Olivia! Patty hadn't heard her come over.

"Look at her," Olivia continued. "She's all inky-colored, and wasn't Ursula an octopus? It fits."

Patty kept her head down to hide her smile. She didn't even hear the other girls' responses. She didn't care.

If Ariel had turned human to be with someone like Olivia,

Patty might have understood.

***

Eager to see Ursula—and Olivia—again, Patty asked her mom to drop her off at school a couple minutes early the next day. When she entered the classroom, Miss Halloran was still in her coat, setting her bag down on her desk. Patty made a beeline for the incubator, not even stopping to hang up her things. She was counting chicks to see if any new ones had hatched when she saw it.

Puffball, the oldest chick, was lying at the bottom of the incubator, covered in blood. A black, tarry streak stained the floor beside her, and Ursula hunched over the body. At first, she seemed to be nudging Puffball, but after a moment, it became obvious: she was pecking her.

"Morning, Miss Halloran." Anna slung off her backpack at the door. "Any new chicks?"

Anna had named Puffball. She'd be heartbroken when she saw what happened. For the briefest moment, Patty was glad—Anna deserved a little heartbreak—but as soon as she thought it, she wanted to take it back. Puffball had died. This was about more than Anna.

"I haven't had a chance to look," Miss Halloran said as Anna crossed the room. "Patty, are there—"

Anna reached the incubator and screamed, spinning toward Patty. "Ursula killed her! Your chick killed her!"

"You don't know that!" Patty said.

"What's going on?" Miss Halloran asked, stepping between them. She looked inside the incubator and clapped a hand to her mouth. "Girls, please, go sit down. I'll take care of this."

"You're getting rid of Ursula, right?" Anna asked, not moving.

Patty froze. She hadn't considered that Miss Halloran might do anything with Ursula. "You can't!"

"Nothing is happening to Ursula right now," Miss Halloran said, returning to her desk for some tissues.

"But she's a murderer," Anna said.

"We don't know that. She could have started pecking at Puffball after she'd already died." Miss Halloran gathered Puffball up in her tissues, wrapping her carefully so no part of her was visible.

"Told you," Patty couldn't help but say.

Anna ignored her. "So you're just going to leave her in there to do it again?"

"We'll keep a close eye on her," Miss Halloran said. "If we think she's trying to hurt the other chicks, we'll separate them, but not until we have more proof."

Patty glanced back down at Ursula, afraid she'd already be pecking another chick, condemning herself, but she just stood alone and preened. Anna must have been wrong. Ursula wouldn't hurt anybody.

***

Patty never went to school early again. Every morning, she dreaded coming in, worried another chick would be dead and Ursula blamed for it. Oddly, more chicks did die, but aside from more tarry black streaks, the bodies were untouched. After a while, Patty worried less that Ursula would be blamed and more that she would also die, but she never did.

In a few weeks, she was the only chick left alive, and the first clumps of permanent fluff started to replace her black baby down.

Miss Halloran explained that Ursula was a Silkie, a type of chicken with feathers that lacked spines and therefore looked like fur. Her siblings would have had the same feathers if they'd survived.

Anna and her friends seemed convinced that, despite the lack of evidence, Ursula had killed the other chicks. Pretty soon, Patty was the only student who still spent time with Ursula. That was okay, though. Patty knew what it was like to be shunned by the entire school. Now, she and Ursula had each other.

"How's the murderer?" Anna asked one Friday afternoon.

Patty was kneeling by the Rubbermaid tub where Ursula lived. She spent every recess there, and it had been about a week since anyone had last bothered her. She'd hoped Anna had found something new to keep her busy, but apparently not.

When Patty didn't take her bait, Anna continued. "Got any plans for when your little friend grows up?"

The question caught Patty off-guard. "What do you mean?"

"People eat chicken. Duh."

"People eat fish, too, but not the kind you keep for pets." Patty jerked her head toward the goldfish in the tank nearby.

"Obviously. They're too small. But they don't make chickens that are just for pets. Miss Halloran got the eggs from a farm, right?"

Patty's stomach started to hurt.

"I heard her talking to the principal," Anna continued. "We're only keeping Ursula because the other chicks died. Otherwise, she'd have sent them all back already."

"She would never!"

"If you ask me, she feels bad taking away the only living thing that ever liked you. Doesn't mean we'll keep her forever, though."

"Ursula's ours," Patty said. "You're making this up." Even so, she imagined herself on her knees, begging Miss Halloran not to send Ursula to her death.

"Don't look so upset. You love chicken, don't you? I bet Ursula would taste great fried."

"She's my friend." Patty had just eaten chicken last weekend. She didn't think she could eat it again.

"You say that now, but you get hungry enough, you'll change your mind." Anna turned away to watch the fish. "The fatties always do."

Patty leaned over Ursula's tub, her vision blurring. "I'm not going to eat you. Friends stand up for each other." If only someone would stand up for Patty.

I will. The words appeared in Patty's mind like a thought, like the *yes* she'd heard before.

She studied Ursula. "Did you just—"

A loud, glassy crash erupted beside her, followed by a scream and the cool sensation of water seeping into her skirt. She stood.

Somehow, the fish tank had fallen over sideways. Cracks spiderwebbed the glass where it hit the counter. Anna stood hunched in front of it, her uniform soaked through as multi-colored pebbles tumbled onto her shoes.

"Anna, what happened?" Miss Halloran asked, rushing over. "Are you okay?"

Anna answered by bursting into tears.

"The fish!" someone yelled.

Gold shapes writhed on the floor. The dark grey tile glistened, the water turning it black like a coat of ink. Back in her tub, Ursula scratched at her wood shavings, undisturbed.

"We need water," Olivia said, hurrying toward the sink.

"Are you hurt?" Miss Halloran asked Anna.

Anna shook her head.

Miss Halloran turned toward Patty. "Did you see what happened?"

"I was playing with Ursula and heard a crash. I wasn't watching Anna."

"I didn't do anything," Anna wailed.

"Patty probably knocked it over on her," Ronnie said from the crowd. Everyone had gathered around to gape at them.

"I wasn't anywhere near it," Patty said.

"It's too heavy for someone to knock over." Olivia approached with a cup of water in each hand. "It must have been a freak accident." She offered one of the cups to Patty. "Help me?"

Patty hesitated. For just a moment, she'd been sure Ursula was communicating with her. Still, whatever was happening, she wasn't going to figure it out with her whole class staring at her. Besides, she wanted to help the fish; even more so, she wanted Olivia to see her helping the fish.

"Sure." Her fingers brushed Olivia's as she took the cup.

***

That weekend, Patty thought of nothing but Ursula. The more she relived those brief moments, those foreign thoughts, the more certain she was: Ursula could talk. But if that were true, what else could Ursula do? Had she somehow knocked the fish tank over? Anna couldn't have done it—she wouldn't have even wanted to—and the tank should have been too heavy, anyway. Really, Ursula knocking it over with magic powers made the most sense. Patty couldn't wait to see her on Monday and ask.

Her parents noticed her sudden enthusiasm for school, but she couldn't tell them her theory. She could convince herself Ursula was magic, but a grown-up? They'd think she was insane. Instead, she told them what they'd most want to hear: she'd made a friend. It wasn't hard to convince them—they'd never understood why her classmates didn't love her like they did.

Finally, Monday came, and she stared at the clock all day waiting for recess, when she'd be free to spend time with Ursula. Miss Halloran had her own plans, however. While the class read their anthologies, she unfurled a huge piece of paper from a roll and taped it to the wall, then laid a plastic tarp out below it.

"We have a new class project," she announced in the minutes leading up to recess. "We're making a mural. Every classroom is making one, and when we're finished, they'll be hung in the hallways together. I'd like everyone to paint something today before you play any games, but don't feel rushed. I'm leaving it up all week to give you a chance to finish anything you've started."

Patty would enjoy making the mural more if she could visit Ursula first. Still, everyone else was lining up in front of the tarp. She'd stand out if she didn't join. Begrudgingly, she chose a jar of black paint and found an open spot toward the end of the mural paper. The portrait of Ursula didn't take long, and as soon as she could argue it looked finished, she stepped away. She could perfect it later.

"Done already?" Miss Halloran asked as Patty crossed the room.

Patty stopped short. "I wanted to tell Ursula about the picture of her I just painted."

Miss Halloran smiled, seeming to accept this. "I'm sure she'll love it."

Finally, Patty knelt over the tub. She scooped Ursula up in one hand, holding her close. "I figured out what's going on," she murmured. "You can talk."

Ursula stood on her palm, cocking her head this way and that as she examined their surroundings. Patty had expected a shocked onslaught of thoughts, but instead, she got nothing. Had she been wrong?

"Did you knock the fish tank over?" A direct question. Maybe that would make a difference.

Were you amused?

She gasped. She'd been waiting for the thought, but it was still a shock. "I knew you had powers."

Were you amused? Ursula repeated.

Was she? The prank had been cruel—the fish could have died—but she'd never forget the sight of Anna, soaked through and overwhelmed. That alone made it worth it. "Yes."

Then you'll love this.

She opened her mouth to ask what Ursula meant, but a high-pitched squeal across the room caught her attention. Anna scurried to her feet from where she'd knelt at the mural. The jar of black paint, which Patty must have left open in her hurry to finish, had fallen on its side, leaving a dark pool on the tarp. The stain spreading over Anna's skirt was visible even from across the room.

Patty hid her smile as she turned away from the chaos. School was about to get a lot more fun.

***

In the following weeks, more things went Patty's way. A textbook, stolen while she wasn't looking, reappeared in her backpack right when she needed it. Ronnie teased her for not wearing her sweater, only for Ronnie's own sweater to disappear completely after she took it off for gym class. Spills happened all the time around Anna and her friends, but when Patty knocked a can of Coke off the table, it landed right-side-up, not spilling a drop. Ursula made Patty lucky. The bullying didn't stop, but this made it bearable.

As the weather warmed, the girls started having recess outside. Patty took to carrying Ursula out with her. She'd taken over most of Ursula's care by then, and she worried about what would happen once the school year ended.

"We need to make a plan," she said at recess one day, flopping down in the grass and settling Ursula beside her. "It's almost summer, and I don't know what Miss Halloran has planned for after we leave."

Ursula had grown into a ratty-looking adolescent, her feathers a patchwork combination of baby down, adult Silkie fluff, and the harder quills of developing primaries. With her new feathers, she could lift herself a foot or two into the air, so her Rubbermaid tub had also been traded in for a chicken wire cage. Anna still insisted that, once she became a full-fledged adult, she'd be sold for eggs or meat. Patty didn't want to believe it, but what were the other options? Miss Halloran could take Ursula home for the summer, but would she really take on that much extra work? Besides, hatching the eggs had been the actual science experiment; wouldn't she want to get new eggs and start all over with her next class?

"I'm not going to let anything happen to you," Patty said. "Miss Halloran doesn't get you. She just sees Ursula the chicken. I see Ursula the Powerful."

Ursula scratched at the grass with feathered feet and stabbed at the dirt with her beak. Magic powers or not, she played the part of a regular chicken well.

Patty lay back, staring at the clouds breezing by. "Could you use your powers to make her give you to me? I bet my mom would say yes. She just said I was getting old enough to have a dog soon, but you're way better than some stupid dog."

Silence. Patty sighed. Ursula didn't talk often—it wasn't like having conversations with another person—but this was a big deal. She could die, or they could at least be separated. She should care enough to say something.

"Hey."

The voice startled Patty, and she sat up. Olivia was walking toward her.

"Hi," Patty said, rearranging her skirt. She hoped Olivia hadn't heard her talking to Ursula.

"Anna lost her bracelet." Olivia jabbed a thumb back toward the playground.

Patty snorted. Anna had gloated about that bracelet all day; clearly, Ursula's mind had been elsewhere while they were talking.

"What?" Olivia's eyebrow raised.

"I was just . . . nothing. What about it?"

"Everyone's looking for it. Have you seen it?"

Patty shook her head. "I didn't even know she lost it."

Olivia paused for a moment, staring at her. "What's with you two, anyway?"

"What do you mean?" Anna bullied her. Wasn't it obvious?

"Why don't you ever stand up to her?"

"I tried once. It didn't end well." Anna had arranged things perfectly to make Patty look like the bully. Since then, she'd preferred to stay out of Anna's way—at least, until Ursula came along.

"Well, if you see the bracelet, give it back to her, okay? Her mom's going to kill her. Maybe if you saved her butt, she'd see you differently."

"Yeah, sure," Patty said. Like that would ever happen.

"You never know." Olivia started turning away, then seemed to think better of it. "You don't have a partner for the history project yet, do you?"

"Nope." She planned to do everything herself, like usual.

"Do you want to work together?"

"Be partners?" Was this a trick? Olivia didn't seem the pranking type. "That would be—yeah. Let's do it."

"Great. We can talk about ideas in class tomorrow."

Without waiting for a response, Olivia turned and started back toward the playground. Something about the way her skirt swished around her stockinged knees caught Patty's eye.

"How do you like that, Ursula?" Patty said when Olivia was long out of earshot. "Maybe you're not my only friend, after all."

Ursula raised her head. A fat worm hung from her beak, glistening as it writhed. She straightened her neck and, with a quick jerk, swallowed it whole.

***

For the next few days, Olivia and Patty spent their history block together, discussing their project between jokes and stories. At first, Patty thought it would be awkward, and she waited for Olivia to notice whatever it was about her that everyone hated. She never did. Instead, they kept finding things in common. They both liked to draw, and they watched the same cartoons. Olivia laughed at Patty, but only when she'd said something funny.

At recess, Patty recounted their conversations to Ursula. She never commented, but Patty imagined she must be happy for her.

On the fourth morning of their partnership, Olivia came to class and settled right into the eternally empty desk beside Patty's. In fifth grade culture, the gesture was unmistakable. Olivia was Patty's friend, and she didn't care who knew.

All day, they whispered to each other and passed notes. Patty never thought she'd have the guts to be so disruptive, but she had a lifetime of friendship to catch up on. Class seemed unimportant by comparison.

They caught an occasional glance from Miss Halloran, but somehow, they reached recess without getting into trouble. Maybe it was pity; surely, Miss Halloran noticed no one had taken an interest in Patty before.

"What do you wanna do?" Olivia asked as they filed out into the overcast spring afternoon.

Patty shrugged. She never did much of anything, but she didn't know how to say that without sounding pathetic.

"We could sit on the monkey bars," Olivia suggested. "They're my favorite."

"That sounds nice."

Most of the girls their age played more organized games or sat in the stands around the running track, gossiping. The playground equipment—brightly-colored plastic slides and tunnels, a jungle of silvery monkey bars, and a wooden model train sized to fit small children—was too childish for them to risk their reputations enjoying. Patty didn't care. She didn't have a reputation to protect.

Olivia climbed most of the way up a wall of horizontal bars before hooking her legs and arms through to sit. Patty followed, conscious of every centimeter her skirt rode up as she climbed. She struggled to find a comfortable position, the cold bars digging into her thighs.

"There you go. You got it," Olivia said once Patty settled in.

"Thanks." Patty glanced down, making sure no one could see any part of her they shouldn't. When she tried looking back at Olivia, a nervous jolt ran through her. Studying the scenery seemed safer.

"Do you like roller coasters?" Olivia asked after a moment.

"Doesn't everybody?"

"My sister doesn't. They make her sick. Last time she rode one, she puked and the whole ride got shut down."

"That sounds horrible." Patty could easily imagine the humiliation.

"Everyone at the park hated her. Now she won't go back, even to ride the mellow stuff. That's why I'm asking you."

"Asking me what?"

Patty couldn't help looking at Olivia then. Her blue eyes were bright with excitement.

"To come with me this summer. I won't have a riding partner if she stays home."

"Come with you? Like, with your parents and everything?"

"If you want to."

Patty didn't know what to say. Being school friends seemed like enough of a miracle. Now, Olivia wanted to hang out this summer? This was the best day of her life.

"I'd love to," she finally managed, trying to hide her stupid grin.

"Great!"

"Fatty Patty, enjoying your date?" Anna's voice from behind them was unmistakable. She came around to face them, a horde of girls trailing behind her.

"Leave her alone, Anna," Olivia said. She didn't sound embarrassed or even angry, just annoyed.

"Did you tell her?" Anna's eyes were still on Patty.

"Tell her what?" The metal bar in Patty's hands grew slippery with sweat.

"Patty's not being open with you, Olivia. I'm guessing she didn't mention she's gay?"

"I am not!" Patty yelled, almost losing her grip on the bars. Why would Anna say that? Olivia would think she was gay!

Was she?

"What do you know?" Olivia said. "It's not like she'd tell you if she was."

"She didn't have to. She wrote it all in her notebook." Anna reached behind her and retrieved something from the other girls: Patty's notebook, inky smudges all over its green cardboard cover. "Except she isn't just gay; she's gay for you. Look."

Patty realized what would happen seconds before it did. Anna held up the notebook, open to a page in the back—a page Patty thought no one would accidentally see. On it, Patty had drawn Olivia's name. Everywhere. *Olivia. Olivia Herrington. Olivia H.* There was cursive and block lettering and even an attempt at illustrating the initials like the first letter in a chapter of a fancy book. Patty had thought the doodling was normal, just enthusiasm for her new friendship, even if it was a little embarrassing, but Anna's explanation unsettled her. Maybe there was some truth to it.

"What?" With one smooth motion, Olivia disentangled herself from the monkey bars and dropped to the ground. Her face turned bright red as she stared at the page. "I should go." She turned, hurrying off toward the school in a march that threatened to become a sprint.

The other girls laughed, and Patty wished she could disappear. She tried to dismount the monkey bars with the same grace as Olivia, but her ankle caught, and she lost her grip, toppling face-first into the dirt. The laughter grew hysterical. She pushed to her feet and ran.

The wooden model train sat on the farthest edge of the school-yard. Patty hadn't fit in it for years, but with only the older kids currently outside for recess, it was deserted. She ducked behind it and curled up in the grass to cry.

After a moment, wings flapped past her head, and something light brushed against her arm. *What's wrong?*

Ursula.

Patty sat up. She'd been so distracted spending the day with Olivia that she'd completely forgotten to bring Ursula outside. Someone else must have done it, but if they hadn't, she'd have been stuck in her cage all day.

"I'm so sorry." Patty dropped her face into her hands. "I ditched you for Olivia, and now she hates me. Everyone hates me but you."

Forget them.

A wet ripping noise cut through the air like something from a nightmare. Patty dropped her hands. Ursula still stood in front of her, but her eyes were dull and lifeless, and her skin sagged on her frame. No, more than that. It was splitting right down the middle. Something pale shone through. Patty felt lightheaded. Was that Ursula's skeleton?

The gap in Ursula's skin widened, and whatever it was inside her moved. Patty slid backwards, scooting on her butt until she hit the train's wooden wall. Her mouth opened to scream, but she couldn't. She could only stare.

Finally, a girl unfolded herself, shrugging off the remains of Ursula's skin. She was smaller than Patty—just like the other girls in her class—but still many times bigger than a chicken. It shouldn't have been possible. Her face was the pastel shade of shadows on snow, framed with hair as black as Ursula's feathers had been. Wispy black fabric wrapped around her body, absorbing all the light that touched it. Her eyes were black, too, with no visible iris or whites, though Patty could still feel them staring.

"Patty," the girl said, her voice smooth as water lapping at the shore. "It's me, Ursula."

Patty scrambled to her feet, acutely aware of the model train stretching away on either side of her, penning her into this corner of the schoolyard. "Ursula was a chicken," she said.

"A chicken who could talk. You believed that, but you can't believe this?"

"What is this?"

The girl extended her arms out on either side of her body and twirled. "This is me."

"I don't understand."

"Chicks grow inside eggs, right? Well, I was inside the chick's body, growing. Today, I was ready to hatch."

It didn't make sense—chicks had organs inside them, not

girls—but the longer Patty looked into the dark mirrors of Ursula's eyes, the less she needed it to make sense. "You're the one who made all those things happen. Not a chicken. You."

"It was both. *I* am both."

"Does that mean you'll go back to being a chicken at some point?"

Ursula tilted her head, accentuating the curve of her cheek. "Do you want me to go back to being a chicken?"

Patty had always noticed angular faces on girls. She'd assumed it was jealousy—her own face was so round—but now she wondered if there was more to it. Attraction? "No," she said, "but why do you care what I want? Why me? Why not one of them?" She jerked her head in the direction of the other girls.

"You were alone. You were the one who needed me."

Patty crossed her arms and looked away. "So it's not about me as a person. It's about my situation."

"Just like Olivia. You thought you had a chance to be her friend because she hadn't spent the past six years of her life mocking you. She could have been anyone."

Was that true? Had there really been nothing special about Olivia?

"See?" Ursula said. "Desperation. You and I have that in common. We both just want the chance to show someone who we really are." She gestured to her human-like body, her long, unruly hair and shining black eyes. Patty could lose herself in those eyes.

"I think I'm gay." Patty hadn't planned to say the words. She'd just opened her mouth and there they were.

"Another reason those girls will never accept you."

Ursula was right. Now that Patty knew the truth, she didn't

want to hide it, but school was already so awful. She didn't need another reason to be singled out. "What do I do?"

"That's simple. Leave."

"Like switch schools?" She'd considered asking to do this before, but it seemed unlikely that public school kids would be any nicer to her. Besides, her parents paid a lot to send her to Seaside Prep. She didn't want to seem ungrateful.

Ursula shook her head. "Like disappear. Leave all this behind you. Forever."

"All of it?"

"That's what I'm doing. Can you imagine what anyone here would say if they saw a girl like me?"

"But my parents."

"What about them?"

"I don't want to leave them. They love me." Patty imagined coming out to them. They'd always accepted her for who she was before. She was sure they'd do it again. Maybe they'd even accept Ursula if Patty explained everything.

"Do they know how people treat you here?"

"Kind of." She tried to spare them the details, but they'd definitely noticed she had no friends.

"And they still make you face that every day? That's not love."

Patty wanted to say it was more complicated than that, but staring into Ursula's eyes, she wondered if maybe it wasn't.

"Come with me." Ursula reached out a hand, pale blue palm up and inviting.

"Where will we go?"

"Anywhere. Everywhere. So long as we're together."

Patty wiped her sweaty palm on her skirt, thinking. Just as she started to reach out, she heard it—someone was calling her name.

"Patty, where are you?"

She spun around, breaking eye contact with Ursula. At her height, she could just see over the train. Olivia had come back outside and was wandering the playground, calling for her.

"Sorry I ran off," Olivia yelled. "I was just surprised. Please come out so we can talk."

After all that, Olivia still wanted to be friends? Patty opened her mouth to respond.

"Before you do that," Ursula said, cutting her off, "know that if Olivia comes over here, I'm leaving. I can't be seen by anyone but you."

"She might understand—"

"She could barely handle a few doodles."

"Fine. Can I meet you somewhere later?"

Ursula's silence was answer enough. "I'm sorry," she said after a moment, "but once I leave, I'm not coming back. You have to decide now. Her or me."

Of course, the decision was more complicated than that, but Patty had always wanted a friend more than anything. Now, she was faced with two very different friends, two very different lives.

Olivia was a normal girl, but she seemed to genuinely want to be Patty's friend. They'd had so much fun in school this week. With her, Patty might actually enjoy living a normal life.

But maybe not. Olivia had run away so easily. Now, she wanted to apologize, but even as she looked for Patty, she smiled at everyone she passed. Surely, she'd act the same way if she'd offended one of them. She was trying to apologize because that was her personality. It didn't mean they'd stay friends.

"Of course not," Ursula said. She'd responded to Patty's mere thoughts. Patty turned toward her.

The worst part of choosing Ursula would be the sacrifice. Patty would have to leave her parents, her home. But she'd also never go to school again, never be bullied again. And she'd have a guaranteed best friend. Ursula wasn't trying to please everyone—she didn't waste kindness on people who didn't deserve it. No, she wanted to be friends with Patty specifically.

Plus, she had powers. Patty might never meet someone with powers again. Could she forgive herself for giving up her one chance to live a magical life?

She would find her parents again when she was older, and they would understand. Every kid leaves home eventually.

Patty locked eyes with Ursula, all her doubts gone. "Let's go," she said, reaching out a hand. Ursula took it, her skin cool and smooth.

This was it. Never again would Patty feel a dozen mocking eyes on her back. Never again would she be surrounded by hurtful whispers. Ursula would take revenge on anyone that treated her that way.

Ursula pulled her close, and Patty's heart raced. They faced each other, their breath tickling each other's cheeks. Maybe they would be more than just friends.

Ursula's lips parted, opening wider than they should for a kiss. Her arms locked around Patty, her grip too powerful to escape. She bent her head closer, and her smile glistened with sharpened teeth.

ACKNOWLEDGMENTS

Thank you to . . .

Nikki Fernley (formerly Morgan) for the original linocut cover art.

All our line editors, *Meghan Witherow-Hunt, Nicole Sly, Amber Lockrow,* and *Christine Stockwell* for their proofreading prowess.

And to *Buffalo Street Books* in Ithaca, NY for providing a community space to debut this book.

9 798990 679825